And Yet, You Still Chose <u>Me</u>

Inspired by a true story

by
Kimberly Ray
with
Sharon Chinn

Strategic Book Publishing and Rights Co.

Hardcover version published in 2009.
.Softcover version published in 2012.

Strategic Book Publishing and Rights Co.
12620 FM 1960, Suite A4-507
Houston TX 77065

ISBN: 978-1-62212-060-4

Cover Design by Garrett Rountree

Book Design by Bruce Salender

Dedication

This book is humbly dedicated back unto the Lord for instilling in me the strength and tenacity to triumph over extraordinary odds. It is also dedicated to those men, women, boys and girls whose silent cries have not been heard. I am hoping that *my* story will encourage and challenge *you* to join me in exposing those dark secrets, past or present, that you've kept hidden deep within, and that you will embrace the gift of forgiveness so that *you* can be launched into *your destiny.*

Acknowledgments

I would like to personally thank my husband Shawn, and my children, Lamont, Savanna, and Shawn, who have been with me on this journey for over twenty-six years! Also my aunt, Sharon Chinn, one of the most phenomenal ghost writers around; Sheryl Rountree, who has traveled faithfully with me on this journey from day one; Andrzej Barkowlak, Takashi Bufford, and Venus Christiansen, for believing in this story enough to share with the world! Also Bishop Millicent Hunter, Belinda Harris, Nina Baker, and Holly Hill. Friends, family, and fans of this book, I could not have gotten this far without your prayers and support! Thanks, and I love you all!

Sincerely,
Kimberly Ray

Chapter 1

As I looked at the white sheets *He* had placed around the sides of the canopy bed where *He* had laid me down, *again,* I thought of the white wings of angels and the white robes of the church choir. So I wondered, in my child's mind, why *He* used these white sheets. White symbolizes purity and goodness, and to curtain *this* place in white is a blasphemy because of the evil acts that he committed against me; perverted acts that robbed me of my childhood innocence. Did *He* think, in his twisted mind, that the white sheets would sanctify his deeds? To this day, I have no answer for that question.

I remember the first time it happened. I was about three years old. My mother, my older sister, my brothers and I had moved from Detroit to Randall, Maryland. My mother had a sister there, whose husband was away serving in the military. Aunt Louise welcomed us with open arms into her home, but for what turned out to be only a short time. My mother had separated from, and was divorcing, my father, Henry MacDonald, in Detroit, so her sister's invitation was exactly the new start that she needed to go on with her "life-after-divorce."

Randall was a beautiful suburban community with lovely homes. The older homes had charm and character only livin' and lovin' can give them, and they were surrounded by stately, lush trees and rolling, grassy hills. There were also several newer subdivisions which included ponds, children's parks and walking and riding paths, all within walking distance. This charming little town was so different from the rough and tumble neighborhood where we had lived in Detroit that it seemed to almost be a *magical* place to my three-year-old, imaginative mind. You see, I had never really seen, let alone lived in, a place like this. A place where all you could hear in the early morning was the sound of birds chirping and sprinklers quietly whirring, as they gently watered the neatly manicured lawns sparkling in the rising sun. And where at night you could hear the sound of crickets, rather than the sirens of police cars or ambulances, so common in our old neighborhood.

My aunt's home was in one of the newer subdivisions. All the walls were pristine white, but her furnishings were bright colors that filled the house with warmth and life. Aunt Louise had no children of her own, so she was excited about having four children at one time to cook for, tell stories to and to love. I had never been happier in my life!

But, as it turned out, my life in that magical place was much too fleeting. It all changed when my mother fell in love with *He*. One day, my mother brought *He* to my aunt's house and introduced him as a new friend of hers. *He* was very tall, at least 6'3", with very dark skin and thick, lighter-colored lips. *He* was also as skinny as he was tall, and I noticed, right away, that the whites of his eyes were almost yellow, like some black cats I had seen in scary movies. Needless to say, his appearance alone frightened me, though he had done nothing to me, at that time, to warrant my fear. Soon, *He* began to come around more and more often, and my mother and *He* very quickly became "a couple."

Then my magical world really began to crumble when my aunt announced that she and my uncle were being reassigned and would be moving to California. They had to make their move within a month, so my mother and *He* decided to move in together in a townhouse. From that point on, life, as I had known it, no longer existed. I called him *He* because I was too frightened of him to call him anything else. The initial fear that I felt became justified almost immediately after we had moved into the townhouse. *He* became the "stepfather from hell," who ruled our household, including our mother, through cruelty and intimidation. My mother, who was a single parent trying to raise four children—two girls and two boys—surely believed that *He* would give her the help and support she needed. However, she was in love with *He*, but *He* fell in love with *me*, at least with my body. To this day, I wonder what it was that *He* found attractive about a powerless, little child. I'll never know, I guess, because only sick, depraved minds and spirits could conjure such thoughts.

My mother worked different shifts at Drysdale's Discount Mart, sometimes during the day, and sometimes at night. I don't remember whether or not *He* worked. All I remember is that *He* seemed to always be at home when my mother was gone. On this particular day, after my mother closed the front door, leaving for work, *He* looked up at me from the bottom of the staircase and made his way up towards me. His dark hands were extremely large, and seemed to always be in need of lotion. The large knuckles on his hands were cracked, and very old and worn-looking. When *He* reached the top of the staircase, *He* stood there with his bathrobe half open, so that you could see the mass of hair on his chest. His appearance frightened me so much that I was terrified of him. His eyes seemed even yellower than I had ever seen them, and they reflected what I soon came to know as *lust*, as well as, I realized later, *hatred* for me, all at the same time.

7

As *He* walked past me, at the top of the stairs, *He* placed his hands on my shoulders with the slightest touch. Then, *He* made his way to the bedroom that *He* shared with my mother, and reached for one of his favorite record albums that was stored in a gray crate with the rest of the albums. I turned to look to see what *He* was doing and saw him blowing the dust off the top of the album cover. I watched the dust hit the hard, wooden floor, and it reminded me of snowflakes hitting a snow-covered ground. He began to play his favorite song on the record player, and, to this day, that song brings tears to my eyes and knots in my stomach. The song's melody was, *"Loving you is easy 'cause you're beautiful; and every day of my life, it's all I want to do. La-la-la-la-la, La-la-la-la-la...,"* or something like that. Little did I know, on that first day, that this would be the song *He* would play every time *He* molested me. *He* reached down, lifted me up in his arms, and carried me to the bathroom. Then *He* placed me back on my feet and removed my panties. Next, *He* reached for the jar of Vaseline. I watched his every move as I stood there with one finger in my mouth, too young to realize his very next touch would change my life drastically. *He* opened my legs in the bathroom and dipped his fingers in the Vaseline. Slowly, *He* placed his fingers between my womanhood (really, my very young childhood, at the time), and rubbed it with Vaseline. Then *He* grabbed my hand and led me to the third bedroom at the top of the stairs. *He* lifted me up in his arms and gently laid me on the bed. (Isn't it ironic that *He* was so gentle before *He* violated me and took away my innocence?)

Suddenly *He* left the room for a brief moment. When *He* returned, *He* had my older brother and sister with him and proceeded to position them at the doorway of the bedroom, where they could plainly see everything *He* did to me. *He wanted* them to see everything that happened, and made them watch! *He* turned back to me and removed all his clothes, as *He* made his way down on the bed, next to my bare body. Even though *He* seemed to always smell like alcohol, because *He* drank *all* the time, the stench, which seemed to come from every pore in his body, was even stronger to me at that moment.

My brother and sister watched from the doorway, too afraid to try to stop him, for we all had been recipients of his brutal cruelty and anger that would come out of no-where for no apparent reason at all. These "punishments," as *He* called them, ran the gamut from physical beatings with extension cords to extreme mental and emotional harassment and abuse. So I understand, as children, why my older sister and brother felt helpless to stop what we all knew, even *me*, at that young age, *He* was about to do.

Then *He* proceeded to do things to my body that only the Lord knows. I remember, vividly, the extreme pain *He* wrought upon my young body, which all my silent tears and cries of resistance could not stop. Just imagine the worst possible sexual violation to anyone's body that you can conceive, and you will barely scratch the surface of the sadistic torture and pain that I endured, and the paralyzing fear I felt. I wanted to scream to the high heaven for some-one to save me and deliver me from the most searing agony my young body had ever experienced. It felt like a knife had ripped my insides apart. The closest I can come to de-scribing this pain is the pain a woman feels in childbirth. But, remember, I was only *three years old*! There I was, tears rolling down my cheeks, too afraid to cry out loud, because *He* might hurt me even more. So, I kept my fingers in my mouth, muffling what would have been very loud cries for help, hurting beyond description and terrified to the point of being petrified.

Can you imagine? Can you fathom how decadent, base, and evil someone would have to be to commit such un-speakable, heinous acts as this? Will you walk in my shoes, a moment, and become three-year-old me, Shelley Mac-Donald, experiencing this for the first time? Unconscion-able, isn't it? And yet, it happened to me!

When *He* finished, *He* picked me up and carried me to the bathroom. With a wet towel, *He* wiped the blood away from my womanhood. Yes, I was bleeding profusely, but that didn't seem to bother him at all. Then *He* said, "Y'all go to your rooms and be quiet," in the deepest, cruelest, most sinister voice I had ever heard. We all scattered like scared rabbits immediately after *He* gave us our marching orders. I went to my room and curled up in a corner, trying to be as quiet as I could be, and within about 15 minutes, though it seemed like hours, I heard him snoring loudly. I slowly got up, still in incredible pain, and tiptoed to the bathroom. Just as slowly, I closed the bathroom door, but with every move of the door, it seemed to creak louder and louder. I just knew the noise from the door would awaken him, and I was so scared it would. But, after I finally got the door shut, I stood very still and listened for any movement from him. Thankfully, all I heard were the uneven sounds of his breathing, as *He* snored. I climbed up on the toilet seat cover so I could reach the wash basin, since I was still too short to stand on the floor and reach it. Then I wet a towel, and began wiping myself over and over and over again. I screamed out, "Mommy, help me!" But my mommy wasn't there. Even if she had been at home, she would not have heard me, because I was screaming only in my mind. I knew I still had to be quiet, so even the tears, which were streaming down my face in such abundance that I could barely see, were silent tears. I felt so unclean and so confused – emotions I had never really experienced in my young life. What was I supposed to do next? I knew that I really couldn't tell my mommy what happened, because we all knew what his "...Be quiet" really meant – "Don't say anything about this to anyone."

Still standing on the toilet seat, I looked at myself in the mirror, and saw that my face was totally wet and red, and my eyes were swollen from my silent weeping, so I wet the towel again and began to wipe my eyes and face. When I looked in the mirror, *this* time, I saw this girl, or woman, I couldn't tell which, at first, standing in the bathroom with me. I almost fell off the toilet seat when I saw her! She walked towards me and said, "Baby Girl, I know that you're hurtin' right now, but it's gonna' be alright. Trust me." I was frightened, at first, because I had never seen this woman before. I guess she sensed how scared I was, because then she said, "Listen, Baby Girl, my name is Jackie, and I'm gonna' always be here with you, even when you don't see me. And I'm gonna' always love you." She spoke in a slow, easy manner, with a cadence that sounded like just a hint of a Southern drawl. But there was also great strength and confidence, combined with warmth and compassion, in her voice. Then she cupped my chin in her hand, gave me a kiss on my cheek, and hugged me close for what seemed the longest time. I still couldn't bring myself to say anything to her, because I was so traumatized and hurt from the assault on my body from *He*, but Jackie just held me in her arms, rocking me back and forth, until the pain slowly ebbed away, and I surrendered totally to her embrace, holding on to her as if my very life depended on it. Then she said, "Now, you go on in your room and rest, Baby Girl, 'cause you need it, and I'll see you again soon. But know that I'll never be far away from you." And she left, just as suddenly as she had come. I slowly tiptoed toward the bathroom door, opened it, creaking sound and all, and rushed to my room. I lay down on my bed, and before I knew it, I fell into a deep sleep.

That night, when my mommy came home, she called me to dinner, but I was only able to eat a little bit. I told her I just wasn't very hungry, and that I was sleepy. She told me I could go to bed, if I wanted to. So I did, and once again, fell into a deep sleep from sheer exhaustion caused by the day's monumental distress and suffering.

The next morning, I woke up with a feeling of utter fear, dread and foreboding (emotions no three-year-old should ever experience). I stayed in my room as long as I could, after I had bathed and clothed myself. Then I heard

Mommy yell at me, "Shelley, c'mon down here and eat your cereal right now. You know I have to leave for work." I did as she said, but could only eat one or two spoonfuls of Frosted Flakes, which was my favorite cereal. Mommy said, "Girl, what's wrong with you? Hurry up and get through." I told her that I had a stomachache and couldn't eat anymore. She quickly felt my head to see if I had a temperature. Satisfied that I was not feverish, she asked, "What have ya' been eating? Did ya' eat too much candy or somethin', even though I've told you kids not to do that?"

Before I responded to her, out of the corner of my eye, I saw *He* glaring at me, as if to say, "Ya' better not say anything about what happened yesterday, if ya' know what's good for ya'." I also saw the terrified looks in my sister and brother's eyes, as, it seemed, all eyes were focused on *me*. So I assured Mommy that I had not eaten anything I wasn't supposed to. She gave me a teaspoon of Pepto Bismol, which was her remedy for all stomach ailments, and told me to go back and lie down until my stomach felt better. I was so relieved to be able to run back to my room, away from his mean stares. I just curled up on my bed like a baby, cradling my body that still ached all over from his intrusion the day before. I began rocking my body back and forth, just as the lady, Jackie, had done with me yesterday. And thinking of her warm embrace, I started drifting off to sleep, still exhausted.

I don't really know how long I dozed, before I heard him come into my room and tell me to go into the bathroom. Mommy had left for work, by then. I started shaking all over, uncontrollably, remembering the pain I had experienced, and I was full of apprehension that I would experience it again. Well, I was right about *that*, because *He* did exactly the same thing that *He* had done the day before, including using the Vaseline, playing that record that I grew to hate, and stationing my brother and sister at the doorway of the bedroom, ordering them to watch while *He* ravaged my body. Just as before, *He* washed me off, went to bed, and went to sleep. I went back in the bathroom, after *He* fell asleep, and, again, began scrubbing my body so hard, this time, that it's a wonder I didn't break the skin. I was trying so desperately to feel clean again. "Baby Girl, what're ya' tryin' to do, rub all the skin off your bones?" Then she flashed the biggest, brightest smile I had ever seen – bright enough that even in the mirror, I could tell it could light up the sky. "C'mon, now. Sit down and let me wash ya' off good." When I heard that voice, it was as if angels had come down from heaven to rescue me. I turned and looked, and she was back! The lady, Jackie, was back! I fell into her outstretched arms and wrapped my arms and legs around her body. She held me tightly, as she walked around the floor of the bathroom holding me, stroking me, and softly chuckling. Then she stood me up on the toilet seat, washed my face and wiped away my tears, and began to gently bathe the rest of my body.

As she bathed me, I couldn't keep my eyes off her. There was no way for me, at my age, to guess her age at that time, but if I were to hazard a guess *now*, I'd say she must have been between 30 and 40, though she could have been younger or older. It's truly hard to say, because she had such an ageless quality about her. Her skin was a beautiful, copper color, and as smooth as silk. She had high cheekbones, which were wonderfully high-lighted with just the right amount of peach/bronze blush. Her hair was almost auburn, but, depending on how the light shone on it, it also had a golden cast. She had a magnificent head of hair, which was full, wavy and curly; and she wore it just below shoulder length. But it was her eyes that transfixed me. Her eyes were so mesmerizing – deep, dark brown eyes that lightened to a hazel shade, depending on the angle of the light and your gaze. The whites of her eyes were the whitest you could ever imagine seeing, even compared to the cleanest white you've ever seen or experienced in snow, bright, bleached white sheets or towels, and – well, you get the picture. And her eyes glimmered, as if little 4th of July sparklers were always going off in them. As if that weren't enough, those gorgeous eyes were surrounded by the longest, curliest natural eyelashes, which were brought to absolute perfection by just a touch of mascara. Jackie wore a beautiful, burnt orange dress, which came just to the middle of her knees and clearly accentuated her curvaceous body and shapely legs. Her dress was accented with a deep purple or grape-colored scarf and belt, and she wore large, gold, hoop earrings with a matching gold wrist bracelet. I thought she was the most beautiful woman I had ever seen. Her spiked-heel shoes were multi-colored, including the colors of her outfit, and she carried a large, burnt orange, leather purse. Though her high-heeled shoes made her look like she was six feet tall, I would guess, now, that she was about 5 feet 7 inches tall, and weighed about 125 to 130 pounds. She had a small waist, voluptuous breasts, and full, rounded hips. (Then I remembered that yesterday, when I first saw her, she wore a bright yellow dress with green accessories and matching shoes and purse. So, I concluded that she must have liked bright colors.)

When she finished bathing me, she reached for her large purse and pulled out of it a huge, fluffy, white towel. Then she wrapped that towel around my body, and, to my amazement and delight, it covered me completely, from head to toe. That towel felt so warm, as if it had just been taken from a dryer, that I didn't want to take it off, because it felt so good. So she let me stay wrapped in the towel a little longer, as she sat down on the toilet seat and placed me on her lap. "He did it again, didn't he? I was there. I saw it, and it was all I could do to keep from tearin' all the *black* off his sorry behind! But, Baby Girl, I'm not here to deal with *him*. That will happen in time. Like I told ya' yesterday, I'm gonna' always be here just for *you*. You hear me? Just for *you*!"

And with that, she reached for her big, burnt orange, leather purse, again, and pulled out a small bottle of lotion. "This is my favorite lotion, 'cause it has the scent of some of the most exotic flowers, plants, and herbs from West Africa that you'll ever find. And what these wonderful plants do is soothe whatever hurts or ails ya'. This lotion also has natural ingredients in it that make your skin feel as smooth as it was when you were a new-born baby. I told you that I loved you. Didn't I?"I shook my head in agreement, still unable to speak. "Well, just to show you how much, I'm gonna' rub your body with this rare, wonderful lotion, and when ya' smell it, from now on, you'll always know that I'm near."

So she began to rub my body with the lotion, and the minute it touched my skin, I began to feel all the pain, all the fear, all the confusion, all the dirtiness roll off my body like waves rolling out to sea after a tide. Then I realized that this wonderful, exquisite fragrance, was what I smelled when she came to me *yesterday*, and I suddenly began to feel very drowsy, again. "OK, Baby Girl, now I want ya' ta' go on and lay down on your bed, like ya' did yesterday, and get you some rest. Because, and I want ya' to remember this all your life, rest is the gift that has been given ta' all of us so that we can wake up each new day, refreshed and full of the strength and energy it takes to handle whatever that day brings our way. No matter if ya' have to deal with really hard things or have the happiest of days, ya' always need your rest to handle it. OK?" Once again, I shook my head in agreement. "All right, now. I'll see ya' again, real soon, and remember that I love you." "I love you, too," I suddenly blurted out. "Baby Girl, ya' just made my heart burst open, 'cause you've made me so happy," she said with that big, gigantic smile that lit up the whole room. Then she gave me a big hug and kiss, and she was gone. I tiptoed to my room, lay down on my bed, and almost immediately fell asleep – only *this* time, I think I had a smile on my face.

Thus began the dichotomous, "Heaven/Hell" essence that was to become the reality I lived on a daily basis for six, long years. Let's talk about the Hell I lived *first*. Every morning, from the top of the staircase, I watched my mother wave goodbye to us kids, with her common-law husband happily by her side, his arm draped around her waist (as if *He* were gracefully ushering her out to work, because *He* supported and appreciated her for working so hard – what a sham!) I watched their every move. I would always hear each step Mommy took, as she crept through the house, preparing herself for work, trying not to wake us. You see, the stairway had no carpeting and the floors were old and scratched up, so everyone in the house knew when someone was up, since every move made was echoed by the creaking of the floor boards. I knew that every step she took meant she was about to leave for the day. I ran to the top of the stairs, with my heart racing, fueled by fear and anxiety, as I watched the person I wanted so badly to be my superhero, my mommy, prepare to leave me, and my brothers and sisters, to the mercy of this monster.

As I stood there, with one finger in my mouth, looking as if my world had just come to an end. I yelled inside, "Please, Mommy, don't leave me with him again." I remember that she had such a sad look on her face, as if there was something she knew. She walked to the front door with her head down, as though shame and sadness filled her heart, and reached for the copper doorknob. (I will never forget that look as long as I live.) Ours was a beautiful home, from the *outside*, and neighbors always saw us as one big, happy family. They never knew what was really going on behind those closed doors. Before she left, my mother looked back at me, seemingly to say something. Something was bothering her, but she said nothing. I didn't understand what that something was, at the time. As for me? I was so scared I felt I *had* no voice. Who could save me from what was about to take place? My superhero, my mommy, had already left for the day. So each day, after my mother left, *He* would follow a daily, and sometimes nightly, pattern of sexually abusing me, and, at the same time, emotionally and mentally abusing all of us kids.

I've got to tell you that I adored my mother. She had beautiful milk chocolate skin, which covered her short, petite body. However her inner beauty was overshadowed by her painful insecurity. Tears began to fill my eyes each day, and trickle down my plump cheeks at the thought of her leaving. I had jet black hair, which was very full and thick. I was always told that I really took after my dad, because I had his light brown coloring and slightly slanted big brown eyes that caused people to call me pretty, little "China Doll" all the time.

My mother usually had a hard time straightening my hair, because I had so much of it. She sat me down in the chair in the kitchen, and turned the stove on high heat, as she parted my hair with a big, black comb. Then she took thick, green hair grease (which is what we called it then— *grease*), and "greased" my scalp and hair, preparing it to be ironed out. Every time I felt the heat of that hot comb come close to my scalp, I jumped! She'd slap me lightly on the side of my head and say, "Shelley MacDonald, if you don't keep still so I kin' get this head of yours done, I'm gonna' smack you!" But I knew that her bark was *usually* worse than her bite, though I was also smart enough to know I'd better not tempt fate and *test* that theory, since, on any given day, I could be wrong about how connected her bark might be to her bite. So I'd try to sit as still as I could until she was finished. (It's funny how you remember little details of your life, and how they affect you, without your even knowing it.)

The *Heaven* that I experienced each day was when I spent some time, however short, with the lady Jackie. She became my mother, my big sister, my friend and playmate, my counselor, my mentor, my confidante – who was always there when I needed her most. I could pour out to her all the pent up feelings and emotions that I could tell no one else. I could vent my anger and frustration about *He,* about my beloved mommy, and about my life, and she would listen with patience and understanding, *most* of the time. But

Jackie would also not suffer me lightly, after a time, when I wanted to go into my pity parties about my life, so I didn't always *like* what she said to me, and I didn't always understand *why* she said them, at that time. For example, I remember one day, after *He* had had his way with me, and Jackie was there in the bathroom with me, the one place where I could find solitude when I was really in deep despair about my life. Jackie said to me, "Now you listen here, Baby Girl!" Then she firmly lifted my chin in her hands and said sternly, "Lift your head up and look at me! Are ya' able to breathe, and walk, and talk? Do ya' have arms, and hands and legs and feet? Are ya' dyin' from some life-threatenin' disease? Are ya' hungry and don't know where your next meal is comin' from? Are ya' dead?" I responded by shaking my head "No." Then Jackie said, "You take that finger out of your mouth and answer me with your mouth, not with your head!" I answered, "No, I mean, Yeah." "Yes to what?" she asked. I meekly answered, "Yeah, I can breathe and walk and talk. Yeah, I have arms and hands and legs and feet." "What about being dead? Are ya' dead yet?" "No," I answered, slightly trembling, and wondering why she was asking me these questions. Then, as if she could read my mind, Jackie said, "I bet you're wonderin' why I'm askin' ya' all these questions, aren't ya', Baby Girl?" I said, "Yeah." "Sweetheart, I'm just tryin' to get ya' to see that there are many people livin' in this world who don't have parts of their bodies, who are hungry, and who are near death with disease, who are makin' it through life with much less than you have, right now. So I want ya' to always remember that no matter how many *bad* things may be happenin' to ya', as long as ya' wake up each day breathin', and you're alive, not dead, ya' have a chance for a better life. So even though we both wish that man wasn't causin' you pain and unhappiness, he still cannot crush ya' permanently as long as ya' have life. Alright, my Sweet? I know this may be hard for ya' to understand, now, but one day you'll see what I mean. Trust

18

me." And I did. I trusted her even without understanding her all the time.

Such was my life for many years, but, believe it or not, it took on a tone of normalcy for me, since it happened day after day after day, and sometimes both day and night. One reason for this state of normalcy was because I allowed my imagination to make me a spectator at this pornographic sideshow, where a little girl, who looked just like me, was the main attraction. I was an observer, just like my brother and sister, not a participant in the show. At least that was how my young mind helped me cope with it all. Though, I still often wondered why this little girl (namely, *me* – Shelley MacDonald) was singled out to be the *star* of the show.

This secret life became the thing that no one dared to talk about in my family. *He* became more and more abusive towards my mother, as well as us children. As I told you before, *He* drank alcohol very heavily, and I never remember him being completely sober. At least two or three times a week, *He* started arguments with my mother. And, when she saw that the argument was escalating, she started making her way upstairs to their bedroom, leaving us kids downstairs. She had enough motherly instinct not to want her children to witness what might ensue. And ensue it would. *He* started arguments with my mother about the slightest little thing.

One day, *He* said to my mother, "Gladys, where in the hell are my cigarettes?" My mother answered in such a low voice that she was barely audible, "I don't know, Phil. Where did ya' have 'em last?" Well, why did she say that? What followed was such a barrage of profanities that you would have thought thousands of dollars had been stolen from him. "What the hell are ya' tryin' to say, huh? Ya' tryin' to get smart with me?" And that's when my mother began edging up the stairs, trying to assuage his uncontrolled anger by saying she would look upstairs for them. *He* followed her up the stairs, berating her with words no adult should hear, let alone any child. Then, invariably, we heard our mother screaming, and heard heavy bumping and thumping and the sounds of slaps and hits to the body – my mother's body, that is. We all cowered there together, each of us wanting to rush to protect our mommy, but we were too terrified to do so. Next, we heard the sound of Mommy's heavy sobs, coming from a place so deep in her that they sounded like the wails and moans of a woman grieving for a long, lost loved one at a funeral. The next day, Mommy, invariably, tried to hide her blackened eyes behind her shaded glasses, and hide her body bruises beneath long-sleeved blouses or shirts. But we kids knew what had happened. We knew what she looked like behind the mask – bruised, battered and bowed. Not only was my mother laden with her current circumstances living with *He*, but also with the path she began, down the road of "low self-esteem," and "low self-worth" from the very day she was born.

You see, as a newborn baby, my mother, Gladys, was thrown into a garbage can by her mother, outside the hospital where she was born. She was quickly found, but spent her young life being raised by a number of people, none of whom were her mother or relatives. Her mother was an alcoholic and never really bonded with her in a mother/daughter relationship. So my mother also spent a good deal of her life growing up on the streets. Then, one day, when she was married to my dad in Detroit, before I was even thought of, she received a phone call that there was a tragedy at her mother's home. When she got there, police were everywhere and escorted her in to see that her mother's body was cut up in little pieces, and the entire house was blood-spattered as evidence of a brutal attack. Her mother had been killed by her stepfather. These less-than-ideal beginnings created a shyness and self-deprecation in my mother that followed her all through her life, resulting in her making extremely bad judgments on the type of men she let take over her life, as well as the type of people with whom she associated, in general. My mother maintained silence

20

about herself for most of her life. She was a product of her generation and the way life was lived at that time, meaning, you just didn't talk about the bad things that happened to you. Rather, you were expected to just "deal with it" and go on living.

So life went on, and we all continued to get up each morning and breathe. And though we had terrorizing moments, sometimes days, we were still kids, and typical siblings – playing together, sometimes fighting, just growing up, the way kids do. My older sister, Dorothy, was very quiet and just kept to herself, most of the time. In fact, she seemed a bit withdrawn, only appearing happy when she was twirling around alone in her room, as if she were a ballerina.

My older brother, Greg, was my idol, at that time. We shared the same father, and, just like me, he looked a lot like our father. He really was quite handsome, and even at a young age, attracted the attention of young girls. Greg was really two personalities. At home, he was the peacemaker, trying to make sure that we kept as quiet as possible when *He* was at home. "Sh-h-h-h, be quiet, you guys. Phil is sleep, and ya' know what you'll get if ya' wake him up," Greg would admonish us, all the while making funny faces that caused us to double over with laughter that we had to stifle by placing our hands over our mouths. He was truly a character, and could be so much fun! But when *He* was up and about, Greg became very quiet, and would try to do everything he could to make sure there was peace in the house, and that we were protected. Sometimes, we imitated and taunted Greg when he was admonishing us, then we'd "crack up" with uncontrollable laughter, even for a short while, though never in front of *He*. At school, Greg was very outgoing, quite different from the way he was at home. He played football and was very popular with both the girls and the boys. He was also a terrific dancer. To this day, Greg is still like a magnet not only for women, but

21

also people in general. Like I said, he was my idol and I really looked up to him as a child.

Last was my little brother, Derrick. Being the youngest child, he was the most adored by my mother. Consequently, he was very spoiled, as the last child in a big family often is. Derrick could do no wrong in my mother's eyes, and when neither my mother nor *He* was around, he really paid the price for being "Mommy's favorite." As siblings usually do, we sometimes nearly tortured Derrick. Mommy would say, "Before I get home from work, y'all make sure ya' bathe Derrick, ya' hear me?" "Yes, ma'am," we'd answer, like obedient children should. And when it was time for Derrick's bath, we'd yell to him, "Derrick, get in here and take your bath!" And that's when the torture began. We took his favorite toy, Oscar (of Sesame Street), and drowned him in the bathtub, which made Derrick scream with despair. Our mom kept rubber gloves beneath the sink, and we would fill the rubber gloves with water and throw them at Derrick, causing him to howl at the top of his lungs. Those were just a few examples of how we made Derrick pay for being "Mommy's Darling." But there were many more.

I remember one infamous "day of torture" for Derrick that I'll never forget. We had gotten Derrick out of the bathtub, and then we tied his hands underneath the washbasin. "I'm gonna' tell Mommy on you," he yelled through rivers of tears, "and I hope she kills alla' y'all!" "Aw, shut up, ya' ain't gonna' tell her nothin', if ya' want us to ever untie ya'," we told him. "And stop whinin'! We're tired of ya' always whinin' about somethin' to Mommy, like a little baby." With that we ran out the bathroom door leaving Derrick sniveling uncontrollably. All three of us were laughing so hard. Then we pulled the bathroom door to shut it tight. When we did that, all of a sudden the doorknob fell off. All the laughter was immediately replaced with sheer panic. We tried every way we could to get that knob back on, but nothing worked. About an hour and a half went by, and we were sweating bullets trying to get that doorknob back on before our mother arrived home to find her "Little Darling" butt naked, tied underneath the wash basin. But nothing worked. Derrick even dozed off, during this time. And then, the time for our "Day of Reckoning" came.

We heard Mommy's key in the front door lock, and got ready to tell the story of our lives. As she did each day, Mommy came in the door and immediately said, "Where's my baby at?" This was because Derrick always ran and greeted her with a big hug, yelling, "Mommy-y-y-y!" The rest of us kids just wanted to barf each time he did this. So we began explaining, "Momma, Derrick kept runnin' through the house, and we were tryin' to catch him to give him a bath. He kept screamin' and hollerin,' tellin' us he didn't *want* to take a bath, so we had to tie him to the wash basin so we could bathe him, Momma. Then we went out to get some more towels, closing the door so he wouldn't get cold, and the doorknob fell off. It locked the door, and we couldn't get it unlocked, so we couldn't get it open." Yes, we lied through our teeth, as most kids, and many adults, do, when they don't want to face the consequences of their actions. She rushed up the stairs, and, somehow, was able to get that door open.

Then Derrick, seeing Momma, started crying and yelping loudly, telling her all the bad things we had done to him. When she turned around and faced us again, after comforting Derrick, her face had the look of some beast getting ready to devour her prey. "Get in here, alla' ya'! Wash your lyin' mouths out with soap until I tell ya' ta' stop! I'll teach ya' to lie to me!" That was the nastiest taste, I believe, I had ever tasted – the taste of bar soap, and I'll never forget it! I don't know how long it lasted, but finally she told us to rinse out our mouths. A sigh of relief, that our punishment was over, came out of all of us. But we were too hasty with our conclusion. "Get in that bedroom, alla' ya', and lay on your stomachs across the bed!" What fol-

lowed was the worst whuppin' any of us had experienced –
ever from Momma! And it was the last time that we tortured our little brother, Derrick. In fact, Derrick and I became very close, after a time. I became sort of a combina-
tion mother/big sister to him, and that closeness remains to
this day.

Those times, when we were just being kids, were wonderful times. But those good times were constantly inter-
rupted by the abuse and terror that *He* inflicted on *all* of us,
which none of us dared to talk about. The only person I
could talk to about what was happening to me was Jackie.
Jackie was my everything. And the neat thing about it is
that she always showed up, in our private meeting place,
my sanctuary, the bathroom, just at the right time, when I
needed her most. I remember that our Christmases were
pretty austere, because we didn't have much money. Each
of us only got one gift apiece on Christmas. The first time it
happened, I wondered why *He* did this, but on Christmas
morning, as we were gathering around a very sad-looking
Christmas tree, *He* said, "Dorothy and Derrick, y'all come
over here and stand beside me. Greg and Shelley, line up
next to Gladys." Though all of us, including Momma, had a
look saying, "Why?" on our faces, we proceeded to carry
out his orders and lined up with the two lines facing each
other, just as *He* had commanded. Then *He* doled out the
gifts one by one, making sure that Dorothy and Derrick got
theirs *first*. This was the beginning of a pattern that was
maintained throughout the years *He* was in our lives –
namely, treating Dorothy and Derrick differently from the
way that he treated my brother Greg and me. Greg and I
were always the recipients of his worst "punishments," as
He called them, even though we hadn't done anything to
deserve them.

On one particular day, we had been riding our Hot
Wheels in the house, which was allowed, as long as we
kept the house neat and spotless. Suddenly, *He* came in the
front door, with that horrible stench caused by too much

24

alcohol, yelling, "Greg and Shelley get yo' butts in here!" Greg and I looked at each other, wondering what in the world *He* be could be upset about *now*. We knew we had been careful not to do anything that would make him or Momma mad. When we went in the room, he said, "Look at this couch. Who moved this couch? One of ya' had to do it, and don't tell me ya' didn't 'cause I can see the imprint of the couch leg in the rug, so I know ya' moved this couch!" Both Greg and I started pleading with him, saying, "But we didn't move the couch, Mr. Phillip. We don't know how it got like that! We weren't even in this room!" Both of us were starting to cry, because we knew what was coming. We just didn't know, at that time, how brutal it would be. "Stop lyin' to me. I'm gonna' teach ya' a lesson to be sure ya' never lie to me again!" Then he grabbed an extension cord and commenced beating my brother and me so hard that we had welts, and our skin broke open so wide that the blood was streaming down our legs, our backs and our backsides. All the while, we were screaming, "But we're not lyin', Mr. Phillip, we didn't do nothin'!" But the more we professed our innocence, the angrier *He* got, and the harder and faster *He* beat us. Then, *He* dragged us in the bathroom, told us to take off all our clothes, ran hot water in the bathtub, and told us to get in the tub. When we sat down in that tub, as *He* had ordered us to do, the pain from that water against those open wounds was so great that we both screamed so loudly it's a wonder the whole neighborhood didn't hear us. But nobody came to our rescue. "Shut that noise up or I'll beat yo' asses more," *He* said. And with that, we tried to quiet down, even though we felt like we were being boiled alive. Some time passed, and *He* finally said, "Greg, git on out of there and go to yo' room. And I'd betta' not hear anotha' peep outta' ya'!" Greg got out of the bathtub, grabbed a towel, and went to his room, still sniveling softly. Then *He* turned to look at me, "I oughtta' leave you in there all night just to teach you that you ain't as cute as you think you are! But yo' momma will be home soon, and I want you to be in bed when she comes, so git on outta' here!"

As fast as I could, I grabbed my towel and rushed to my room. Dorothy and Derrick were still downstairs playing quietly, so I had the room all to myself. I was so sore all over that I thought I would just be better off dead. Over and over this man singled me out, and sometimes my brother, as if he resented that we were fairer-skinned kids. *He* often told us that he was going to be sure to break us down so we wouldn't think we were better than darker-skinned people, like him. *He* had a chip on his shoulder as large as a plank, and, obviously, an inferiority complex about his own skin color. He had a bias about skin color, in general, which manifested by abusing me and Greg. What was so incredible about his perverse thinking was that Greg and I never even *thought* about ourselves in that way – better than anybody else. But the pattern continued for the six years *He* was with our family.

After that beatin' and boilin' incident, I went to my room and truly wanted to run away or die. I felt trapped in a madness that was not of my own making. I thought if I couldn't run away, because I had no place to go, maybe if I just made myself really sick and had to go to the hospital, Momma would pay more attention to what was happening to me, and get rid of *He*. I was trying to figure out all the things I could take to make myself sick, when I suddenly heard, "I know ya' ain't thinkin' what I think ya' thinkin'! I just know I've gotta' be wrong about this. Not after all this time that I've been comin' to ya' practically every day, givin' ya' the benefit of my life's learnin's—buildin' ya' up to be strong in this life, no matter what life brings ya', pourin' out my love and my heart to ya.' I know my Baby Girl ain't ready to just give up!" I couldn't believe it. The Lady Jackie, was here standing in my bedroom! We had always been in the bathroom when she came to me before, so this was a *major* shock and surprise. "Listen, my Sweet. Ya' know I love ya', right? And ya' know I'll always be here for ya'." I shook my head in agreement. "Well, you've gotta' also start thinkin' about and believin' all the things I share with ya' to let ya' know you are strong enough to handle anything that this life hands ya'. I know that S.O.B. so-called man should be tarred and feathered and hung by his balls for what he's doin' to you kids and yo' momma, but especially to *you*, and, believe me, there are people I could call on who would take care of him in a heartbeat! But, I'm not here to do that. I'm here only for you. Now, come on over here and give me my hug, and put away all those thoughts ya' have about runnin' away or makin' yo'self sick. Know this, Baby Girl, in life, ya' cain't really run away from *anything*. Ya' just have ta' pull out all the strength ya' have and take on each day as it comes, no matter how hard it may be. 'Cause, just like I keep tellin' ya', as long as you are breathin', you can always look forward to brighter tomorrows. And, by the way, did ya' stop to think how sad I would be if ya' left me? Do you know how lost and devastated I would be if I couldn't be with ya'?" I hung my head and hugged her even tighter, because I hadn't thought about her when I was so low. "Alright, now. Let's have no more thoughts about leavin' me, ya' hear me?" "OK," I answered.

Then she pulled out that big, fluffy white towel, that never seemed to get dirty, from her purse, and gently bathed my wounded body. Next, she rubbed her healing lotion all over me, and wherever it made contact with my skin, I felt a cool, soothing sensation that immediately extracted the raw soreness and pain from my wounds. "Now, show me those dolls ya' told me ya' play with all the time. Let's have some fun and forget about that crazy man." So I got out my two favorite dolls. One was my Raggedy Ann doll, and the other was just a doll's head with hair, which I named Ebony. I'd play with Ebony for hours, styling her hair. "Ya' like to do hair, too?" Jackie asked, seemingly very pleased. "Girl, give me that doll so I can show ya' some *real* hair styles that you can remember for yourself when ya' get older." So Jackie and I spent the next hour or so in my room, playing with my dolls. She made me forget all the hurt and pain I had experienced that day. And, as was the usual practice each day after *He* molested me, no one disturbed me while I was in my room, or in the bathroom, and I had my Lady Jackie all to myself.

Chapter 2

"Ya'll hurry up and get ready for school," Momma yelled up the stairs. "Ya' know I've gotta' get to work!" So Dorothy, Greg and me scurried around, bumping into each other, snapping at each other, "Get outta' my way," as we each tried to get bathed and dressed for school every morning. Derrick was still too young to be in school, so he stayed at home. It was the same every morning, a three-ring circus, until we heard our mom say, "I ain't gonna' tell ya'll agin' to get down here!" So we all rushed down the stairs at once, buttoning up our clothes, with our shoes not yet completely tied. "Tie those shoes before ya' leave this house. You know better," Momma yelled sternly, especially to my brother, Greg, because he never had his shoes tied. "One of these days ya' gonna' kill ya'self fallin' on those shoestrings 'cause you were too hardheaded to mind me," Momma scolded Greg.

Momma was always dramatic in the mornings, trying to get us kids off to school and herself to work on time. I looked forward to going to school each day, as a little girl; and, as is the case with many kids, *Recess* was my favorite time of the day. I felt free from worries and safe from hurt or harm when I was in school, because I knew that the adults who were responsible for me would not let anything bad happen to me. So, each day, when I got ready to go to school, I could hardly wait to run out the front door, with my brother, Greg, and escape from the house that had been my prison and my torture chamber for so many years. Greg and I went to the same elementary school, Randall Elementary School, and rode on the same school bus each day. We always sat together on the bus, and this morning was no different. Our sister, Dorothy was in middle school, and took a different school bus.

By this time, I was already seven years old, and though *He* continued to molest me daily even *then*, (No – it had not stopped in all those years), for those eight hours that I was in school, I was free from his grasp, his demands, and his control. It was a glorious feeling, because I felt that I was in control, during those eight hours. It was as if I were surrounded by a fortress of protection that *He* could not penetrate—a fortress manned by the adults at the school who were there to protect me. They were my army, and I had nothing to fear. So school became another refuge, where I was allowed to be a child. Because of all that I had endured from *He*, even though I was only seven years old, I felt much older, and much more mature than the other kids my age. It was as if I had been catapulted into womanhood, while still being trapped in a seven-year-old girl's body. But while I was at school, I could still be a child and languish in the kindness and love that my teachers showed each of us. I felt they cared about me, so I could bask in the nurturing they gave me, completely devoid of any fear that their affection would result in any untoward or inappropriate behaviors that would hurt me. I trusted the adults in my school without question, and I was convinced that for the eight hours that I was there, I could be the free, unguarded child I wanted to be.

My homeroom teacher, Mrs. Foster, was the kindest, most cheerful woman I had ever met. She always reminded me of Mrs. Santa Claus, because she had gray/white hair, wore wire rim glasses, was a full-bodied woman, like Mrs. Claus, and was unfailingly warm and chipper. Mrs. Foster kept cookies, apples and other snacks at her desk for us, and used these snacks as rewards for both good class participation and good behavior. Each morning, she greeted me by saying, "Good morning, Shelley. How pretty you look today." I would think *she's just bein' kind.* I thought that because, we were so poor, we hardly ever had brand new clothes. Our mother purchased all of our clothes from Goodwill, and our shoes were sometimes so worn with holes in the soles that we had to put cardboard in the bottoms of them to protect our feet. But Mrs. Foster looked beyond that and made me feel special, anyway.

Every day, the school bell rang at 12:30 p.m., and all of us school kids would bolt out the door to the playground for the recess period. *Recess* – my favorite time of the day! It seemed as if the sun was always shining, and we were free to do whatever we pleased, or at least that's what I felt. Teachers' aides were camped all over the playground, as it was their responsibility to carefully watch us during Recess. I happily played by myself, escaping into my fantasy world full of joy, freedom and safety. I really didn't care that the other kids didn't want to play with me because they thought I was weird or different. They basically ostracized me because of the way I dressed, and also because I was such a loner. They would taunt me unmercifully. Especially Little Jimmy. He was the ringleader and a bully. "Girl, you so strange. You always by yourself all the time. And that ugly dress. You wearin' that same ol' dress agin'," he yelled at me. All the kids gathered around, laughing hysterically. "You'd better leave me alone or I'll get my brother, Greg, to sock you one," I yelled back. "Yeah, right," he'd say, running away, laughing with the other kids. The one thing that I knew was that Little Jimmy was terrified of my brother, Greg. I also knew that my brother Greg would take up for me. So that's how I countered Little Jimmy when he messed with me. I avoided the leers and cruel jeers of some of the other kids by being satisfied to play alone.

Like most days, at Recess, I ran toward the red, yellow and green carousel, which was rusty and barely able to turn. The fact that it was worn and old didn't matter to me, because I could spend time going round and round in my own world, and no one would bother me. I loved my carousel. For me, it represented a whole carnival of rides, where I could fly through the air like a bird and be free! The playground was located toward the back of the school. I ran toward the carousel at full speed, by myself, reaching it first, which was so exciting! I had on my favorite baby blue dress with small round beads on the edges. I could hear what sounded like adult and teenage voices somewhere behind me, but I never looked back, because I knew none of the other kids would be following me. I reached out to touch the bars of the carousel, and suddenly I slipped and fell on my back.

When I looked up, I noticed a young boy coming toward me. He looked to be about 13 or 14 years old, too old to be in our school. I had never seen him before. I noticed that his hair was matted and filled with balls of lint. As he came closer, I saw a look in his eyes that was familiar to me – it was the same look that *He* always had when *He* violated my body and destroyed whatever joy was in my life. The fear that still gripped me each time *He* approached me, filled my very being when I saw this boy's eyes and the look on his face. And though the daily assault on my body had become a type of perverted normalcy for me at home, even though I still feared and dreaded each time it happened, I did know what to expect. But I was at school now – my haven, my refuge. I needn't fear anything here. Right?

When the boy reached me, he pushed me back on the ground, lifted my favorite dress, and raped me right there on the school grounds. At first, I didn't believe it was happening to me. It was as if I was having an out-of-body experience, and I was looking down at this happening to someone else. Looking down, I saw a group of boys gather around and watch, putting their hands over their mouths to subdue their giggles and obscenities as they looked on. Then a second boy raped me, while they continued to look on. I had my eyes closed all the while, and tears plummeted down my face. I felt powerless and was too petrified and ashamed to cry out for help. When I opened my eyes, to my complete surprise, I saw one of the teacher's aides standing there with the kids that were gathered around me. I was so relieved, because I knew she would rescue me, and would make sure punishment would be doled out to those boys responsible! Instead, I noticed an insidious smile on her face, as if she too was enjoying this spectacle. Then she just turned her head and looked the other way. She didn't stop it. She didn't make sure I wasn't hurt. She just stood there and looked the other way while I was being attacked. Next, I began to move my body, because I was feeling the pain of what was happening to me. All the boys suddenly scattered and ran, I guess because when I started moving my body, they probably thought I would get up and yell for help. But the teacher's aide was still there. I looked straight at her, expecting her to help me and comfort me, in some way, even though she had looked away while I was being raped. But what I saw next was a look at least as terrifying as *His* looks. This look clearly said to me, "You'll keep your mouth shut about this, if you know what's good for you!" Then she walked away.

I lay there a minute, shaking with fear, pain and disbelief. Was I dreaming all this? Did one of my protectors, here at my haven, my refuge, really allow this to happen to me? If I did report it, and also report that she was there, would anyone even believe me? After all, I was powerless! I was just a frightened little girl whose whole world had now been shattered. I had no place to go, and no one I could trust here at the school. I got up and ran to the restroom, after these attacks. A girl named Marsha, who was always nice to me, was standing at the wash basin washing her hands. When she saw me she said, "Shelley, what happened to you? Are you alright? Were you in a fight?" "Yeah, but I'm alright," I told her. "Who'd you get in a fight with, Shelley? Did you beat them up?" Marsha asked. "I don't think they go to this school, but I think I got in a couple of good hits," I answered her, still mired in the shroud of silence that plagued me and my family. "Well, are you sure you're alright? Do you want me to go get Mrs. Foster?" "Naw, I'm OK. But thanks anyway." And with that, Marsha left.

Luckily, no one else was in the restroom, or came in while I was there. Then I turned and looked in the mirror. What I saw brought tears to my eyes. My favorite dress had mud stains and grass stains all over it, and there was grass in my hair. I washed myself off, as best I could, trying not to be too late for class. No matter how hard I scrubbed, those mud stains would not go away. They just got bigger. Frustrated, I went into a stall, and just sat there, for a minute, replaying in my mind what had just taken place. "Those little nappy-headed, beady-eyed boys had the nerve to touch my baby. They just don't know who they're messin' with," I heard out of the blue. "Jackie, is that you?" I said, startled, as I jumped up from the toilet seat. "Well, who else do ya' think it would be?" Jackie said in that strong but soulful way that only she could. "Yeah, I'm here, Baby Girl. And I saw those two heathens violate my baby's body. Don't you worry. The day will come when those two rug rats will regret the day they ever saw you. Now, how ya' doin', really?" "Jackie, why did they pick on me? I didn't do anything to them. Why did they do this to me?" I asked, trying to understand. I didn't tell her that the attack on me today made me feel like there was some kind of flashing, neon sign attached to my body saying, "*This is Shelley. You can do anything you want to her. She won't mind, 'cause she's used to it!*" "Now you just heard me call them *heathens* didn't you?" Jackie reminded me. "Heathens don't care about right and wrong like we do, Suga'. They don't have values and morals that keep most people from hurtin' other people. So no matter whether you did anything or not, which you *didn't*, you just happened to be in the path of their wrongdoin' today. Now, let's get ya' cleaned up a little bit more, so you can get to class before you're too late. And I'll see you later." So she helped me clean up a bit more, pulled out that big, fluffy white towel, and wiped me off. Then she pulled that bottle of lotion out of her purse, put just a dab on me, and sent me to class with a hug and a kiss. I was a bit late getting back to class.

I quickly scurried to my desk, trying not to be noticed. But Mrs. Foster saw me come in. She came over to me and said, with concern in her voice, "Shelley, are you OK? Why are you so late to class, and what happened to your clothes?" "I'm OK, Ms. Foster. I just fell off the carousel, and tried to clean myself up. That's why I'm late to class," I answered, softly. "Are you sure you don't need to see the nurse?" she inquired further. "No ma'am. I'm alright," I answered, appreciating her concern, but also wanting her to just go away! Finally, she told me what the class was studying, and I absorbed myself in my studies the rest of the day. The school bell rang for dismissal, that day, and, as I was leaving the room, Mrs. Foster gently pulled me to the side and asked, "Shelley, is there anything you want to tell me? You know you can, don't you?" And as much as I wanted to, I couldn't bring myself to tell her what had happened that day, nor what had been happening for a long time in my home. Maybe I was too ashamed. At minimum, I still was too frightened about the consequences from *Him* if I *did* say anything. "No ma'am. I'm alright," I answered her. And I quickly rushed from the room to meet my brother, Greg, at the bus stop.

He was in line, looking around for me. As I walked up to him, and we were getting on the bus, he looked at me, and frantically said, "Shelley, what happened to your clothes?" I just dropped my head down and said, "I'm alright." We sat down in our seats, and my big brother put his arm around me, comforting me, silently. He cupped his hand under his chin, and leaned his head on the window by his seat, all the while, keeping his arm around me. When I looked at his face, I saw on his countenance a level of frustration I had never seen before, from the deep furrows in his forehead to the tight clenching of his jaw. At the same time, you could hear whispers permeating the air in the bus, saying, "What happened to Shelley? Did you see the dirt all over her dress?" But I drowned out the whispers until all I could hear was a drone. I buried my head on my brother's shoulder, covering my face and my ears with my little jacket, so that I didn't have to see, hear or talk with anyone. I felt so low and so guilty, even though the lady Jackie had told me that what happened was not my fault. I still kept questioning, in my mind, why I was singled out. *Why did those boys think they could attack me, rather than someone like Marsha, for instance? Did everybody know what He had been doing to me for years? Is that why they felt safe abusing me?* I needed to find the answers to these questions, but I didn't know how. So I finally just relaxed under the cover of my jacket, protected by my brother's arm around me until we reached home.

At home I rushed through the door and ran up the stairs, pulling my book bag behind me. Momma was home, cooking dinner in the kitchen. "What's wrong with yo' sister?" she asked Greg. Then something happened that had never happened before since *He* came to live with us. My brother, Greg, turned to my mother and said, "Momma, how long are you gonna' be with *him*?" He was angrier than I'd ever heard him, pointing his finger at *He*, who was sitting at the dining room table, waiting for dinner to be served. It was as if my brother's mind had *snapped*. In that question, all the pent up anger, frustration, resentment, irritation and hatred that my brother had held inside for all these years erupted from deep within the depths of his very soul, like a volcano spewing hot lava. These buried emotions had all been caused by this monster of a man whom our mother had brought into our lives. There was no way Greg could have stopped saying those words at that time, on that day. Because, between the daily abuse I, his beloved little sister, was subjected to, which he was made to watch, and the constant tension in the house whenever *He* was at home, Greg had just had enough. Just *He's* presence was enough to make everyone walk on eggshells. Had the torturous beatings and verbal abuse *He* inflicted on us kids, and the horrific treatment of my mother, reached some kind of ultimatum in Greg's mind? Had my brother Greg, now a man-child, reached his wall, his boiling point, his tolerance level? Also, my brother knew, somehow, without my even telling him, about my abuse at school that day. And with that, combined with the horror of our daily lives, he had arrived at his "Point of No Return," where he just couldn't, and wouldn't, take it anymore!

Greg's anger and resentment was equally directed toward my mother, because she had *allowed all this to happen* for all these years. I was listening from the top of the stairs, and my little brother, Derrick and sister, Dorothy just stopped dead in their tracks, and looked at Greg, dreading what might happen next. Mother yelled at Greg, "Boy, have you lost your mind? Go sit down somewhere," trying, in her own way, to protect him from what she *knew* would be inevitable—a violent attack from *He*! All eyes were on Greg, because none of us believed that he had uttered the words that *all* of us truly wanted to say, but didn't have the nerve to, because we didn't have the courage or the will. Even *He* turned and glared at Greg, incredulously, not believing what he had just heard. Then *He* rose slowly from the dinner table and said, "Gladys, I'll handle this. Let me talk to him, man-to-man." And though *He* had made this pronouncement very calmly, we all *knew* that *He* was raging inside. "C'mon. Let's go upstairs and talk," *He* said to Greg. Then *He* put his hand on my brother's shoulder and ushered him up the stairs. As I saw them coming up the stairs, the look on Greg's face spoke volumes. "Oh, no! What have I gotten myself into now." His look conveyed genuine regret as the gravity of his actions seemed to have sunk in. My mom looked up at me and motioned for me to come downstairs, and I did.

Greg's screams of pain were heart rending. He was yelling, "I'm not a man. I'm not a man! I'm sorry! I'm sorry!" Next, we heard Greg cry out in a loud, piercing shriek, followed by sobbing and wailing, so full of suffering and torment that we all shuddered, including Momma. Then there was silence. The silence was almost as bad as hearing our brother's screams. And we kept looking at each other, wondering, *Is Greg dead? Did He kill Greg? What's going on?* Shortly, thereafter, we heard *He* open the bedroom door. *He* came down the stairs, and sat back down at the dinner table. "He'll be alright," *He* announced to everyone, as *He* began to eat his dinner. After *He* ate and had a couple of beers, *He* finally dozed off on the couch.

Momma, seeing *He* was asleep, rushed up the stairs to check on my brother. She knew she dare not go up there while *He* was awake, or she would have been the next victim. Momma ran to Greg and tried to hold him, but when she touched his arm, he cringed and yelled in pain. "Baby, I'm so sorry," my mother said, trying to comfort him. What she saw next was my brother writhing in pain because his right arm was totally twisted and limp behind his back. Upon seeing this, my mother sprang into action like a mother bear protecting her wounded cub. She grabbed my brother's jacket, put it over his shoulders and said, "C'mon, Baby. Let's get you to the hospital." So, knowing that *He* would sleep for hours, my mother felt safe taking Greg to the hospital. I've often wondered what she told the doctors at the hospital had really happened to Greg's arm. I am certain she *did not* tell them that *He* broke it. More than likely she told them that Greg fell out of a tree, or something like that. And as it turned out, my brother's bravery, fueled by his frustration, resulted in his having a severely broken arm.

My love and respect for Greg grew even greater, after that. You see, my brother had the courage to try to be our family's hero, risking his safety, his health, and even his life by standing up to *Him*. What courage that took! I no longer felt the need to refer to Phil as *He* after he broke Greg's arm. Frankly, in some strange way, even though my brother was hurt terribly because of it, to the extent that he never again attempted to display that level of valor against Phil, his courage inspired me. Of course the source of my own new found strength was my relationship with my lady Jackie. She made me feel even more confident that we would all be OK, one day. The lady Jackie's words kept coming back to me: "Are ya' dead yet? Are ya' still breathin'? Then each day, you wake up breathin', brings with it hope for a better day and better tomorrows." My brother, Greg, had been unmercifully injured, but he wasn't dead yet, and neither were the rest of us. When I went to bed that night, I fell asleep hearing those words from my lady, Jackie, and they comforted me.

Chapter 3

The choir was swaying back and forth, singing that old hymn, *"Soon and very soon, we are going to see the King..."* Yes, it was Sunday, and the whole family was in church, as usual, pretending to be the perfect family, though LIES, DECEPTION and a SHROUD OF SILENCE continued to be our way of life. This was the church Phil was raised in, so, naturally, his loving family, (masked as me, my mother. and my sister and brothers) attended there, as well. His mother and his biological children, from a previous relationship, also attended this church every Sunday. Phil and his mother were very active in the church, and everyone knew them, (or *thought* they did). His children lived in another town, not too far from ours. One of his kids was a daughter, Chelsea, and I wondered if she had experienced with him what I had? We never really got to know his other kids, so I'll probably never know.

Greater St. John's Missionary Baptist Church was a very small church, established in 1956. Inside were a red carpet and hard, wooden pews in the sanctuary. The choir wore red robes to match the carpet, on this Sunday. We always wore our very best clothes to church and on this Sunday, I wore a yellow dress with white patent leather shoes and a matching white patent leather purse. My mother was in the choir singing the solo of "Soon and Very Soon." I stood there in awe as she sang the next verse of this beautiful hymn, *"... We are going to see the King, Hallelujah, Hallelujah..."*

Mrs. Jensen, a fellow parishioner, was so beautiful; not only outside, but also inside, that I'll never forget her. She wore her hair pulled back in a bun every Sunday, and crowned her head with the biggest, most beautiful hats I had ever seen. The hats matched each outfit she wore. She also wore white gloves, and carried a large, lace-trimmed handkerchief, which she placed over any part of her legs that might have been exposed when she sat down. I didn't know the reason then, but now I know that using a large handkerchief in this manner is an expression of modesty and humility in the church, and a further expression of respect for the sanctity of the church, which many church-going women *still* practice *today*. All I knew was that Mrs. Jensen looked elegant, classy and distinguished. This lovely lady walked over to me each Sunday and never failed to say to me, "Sweetie, how are you doing today?" so sincerely that I felt she was genuinely interested in my well-being, and I admired her, almost as much as I loved my lady, Jackie. I had become so distrustful of *any* adult, after that teacher's aide failed to defend me, that Mrs. Jensen had to be *very* special for me to feel comfortable enough to let down my guard, as I did with only her and my lady, Jackie. I always smiled, as I looked up at Mrs. Jensen's gorgeous face, and said, "I'm doing fine," because she made me *feel* fine. I fantasized about being Mrs. Jensen's daughter, and wished I could go home and live with her forever! (Isn't it poignantly sad that it took such a little expression of concern for me, and a show of kindness towards me, to make me gravitate to the person conveying these emotions, to the extent that I even desired to leave my home and family to live with her?) She was one of the bright lights in my life, at that time. Should I ever see her again, I will rush to tell her how very much her gentle words and kindness had touched my heart and how they helped carry me through my week until I could see her again each Sunday.

As the choir continued singing, I felt a peace that I could not explain, but I knew it had something to do with this King named Jesus that they kept singing about, preaching about, giving testimonies about, and praising. Every time the choir sang the praises of this Jesus, something on the inside of me would begin to stir, but I couldn't put this feeling into words. When the choir ended its renditions, and the choir members were seated, the pastor took the podium. Pastor Morris was an older gentleman, probably in his 60's. His father, before him, founded and pastored the church from the beginning, and he followed his father as pastor upon his retirement. Pastor Morris was also what I heard grown-ups describe as a "big, strappin' man."

Our pastor must have weighed close to 300 pounds, and he was quite tall. He had a deep, booming voice that ensured no one would fall asleep in church during his sermons. He also liked to sing, and often broke into song, before, during or after his sermons. And, when he preached, especially toward the end of his sermons, he took deep, long breaths, between passages, as if he was gasping for air. It sounded as if he was making some kind of "whooping" sound when he did this, and sweat streamed down his face, profusely, as he was preaching. Pastor Morris always wore preacher's robes that looked something like the choir robes, but seemed to have a different aura about them. They seemed to demand a kind of respect, by the mere wearing of them, which was at a different level of reverence than the choir robes. He also wore a white collar around his very large neck.

Before Pastor Morris began preaching, and before church service started, the Ladies' Auxiliary of the church made sure there was a small, white towel, and there was a glass of juice, in the pulpit for his use. These ladies were always dressed in white uniforms. Pastor Morris really needed that towel they put out for him, because he continuously wiped the sweat from his face and brow all through the sermon. "I want to ask you somethin', Saints," Pastor Morris began. "Now the choir just sang *Soon and very Soon,* we are goin' to see the King. If he walked down this middle aisle in this sanctuary right now, would you know Jesus? And, just as important, would *he* know *you?*" The congregation began murmuring. "If he should come today, and none of us knows the hour or the day when he'll come, are you ready?" The congregation murmured even louder. "Let's all ask ourselves that here today, because the title of my message today is "Do You Really Know Him – Are You Really Ready?" The congregation responded, "Amen," loudly, almost in unison. "Preach, Pastor," someone else yelled out. Then Pastor Morris referred to some scriptures in The Bible, waited for the congregation to turn to those verses, then had the congregation read them out loud with him. "Father God, let those with ears to hear receive and understand your word to them today. Decrease me and increase Thee here today, Lord, and let the words of my mouth and the meditations of my heart be acceptable in Thy sight, Oh Lord, my Strength and my Redeemer. And let the church say Amen," he enjoined. The congregation responded with "Amen," and sat down.

As I listened to Pastor Morris preach that day, I began to ask myself, "Who is this Jesus, and how do I get to know him? Where can I meet him?" As if he read my mind, Pastor Morris said, "If you don't really know Jesus, if you haven't surrendered your life to him completely, if you know, in your heart, you're not yet ready for his coming, then I want you to quickly come down here and stand in front of this altar." Suddenly, I stood to my feet, and, without a care in the world, walked to the front of the pulpit and started shouting and crying out, "I want this Jesus! I want Jesus!" And there, at the age of nine, I accepted Jesus Christ as my Lord and Savior, though I wasn't entirely sure what all of that meant. I was the only person who came to the altar, that day, but I didn't feel alone. Momma came down from the choir stand and stood with me, with her arm around me, and that was the closest I had felt to her in a long time. Pastor Morris laid his hand on my head and prayed over me, asking me if I accepted Jesus Christ as my Lord and Savior, did I believe that Jesus died, was buried, and rose from the dead and was resurrected, and if I repented of my sins. "Yes," I answered to each question, louder than I usually talked, but still not fully understanding what I was saying "Yes" to.

Then the congregation laughed and clapped, and people started coming up and hugging me. I felt so much love, that day. My mother was crying, but I didn't know why. Somehow I did know, however, that these were not sad tears. Shortly thereafter, I was being ushered back to my seat, and I looked up and saw my lady, Jackie, standing at the back of the church, smiling broadly, her beautiful cheeks soaked with tears. She looked especially resplendent, that day, dressed completely in white, from the dazzling, broadbrimmed white hat on her head to the white shoes on her feet. I started to run down the aisle to her, yelling, "Jackiee-e," but she suddenly put one finger to her lips, signaling me to be quiet. I closed my mouth, and she said, "Baby Girl, I am so happy for you today and so proud of you. One of these days, you'll realize what you've really done here today. I love you, and I'll see you later." Then she blew me a kiss and was gone. I stood there for a minute, just thinking about how stunning she had looked, all in white. The white was so bright, it seemed iridescent. Someone said, "Oh, you sweet darling, I know you're just running for the Lord, now, with joy. I'm so happy for you, too." It was Mrs. Jensen, hugging me. Then Pastor Morris, said, "That's alright, Shelley, you just keep on runnin' for Jesus and runnin' *to* Jesus. Just run all around this church, if you want to. You see, Saints, this little child is showin' us grown folks what true joy in the Lord looks like. We should take lessons from her. Like the good book says, '...and a little child shall lead them.' "Go on, Baby, run all you want."

It was then I realized that when I was running to Jackie, everyone else in church must have thought I was running because of my joy at accepting Jesus. *Jackie must have left too quickly for them to see her,* I thought. So, just as the pastor told me to do, I just kept running around that church, and as I kept running, I began to laugh, because it just felt so good. Well, the organ and drum started playin', and the congregation started laughin' and clappin' and dancin', and Pastor Morris and the choir started singin', *"Victory is mine, victory is mine, victory today is mine...,"* and some of the elders and deacons and mothers of the church started praying out loud in a language I didn't understand. For a small church, there was so much singin' and prayin' and clappin' and dancin' going on in that church that I thought they could hear us all the way downtown! But I didn't care. I just felt free running around that church, and it didn't matter to me if no one else felt that freedom but me. I really don't know how long I ran before I stopped. I just know I was completely soaked with sweat and exhausted when I finished, and I just laid down in front of the altar. I felt someone put a sheet over my body and begin fanning me. I also heard them praying in that strange language over me, as I laid there. After a time, I opened my eyes and stood up. Then I went back to sit in the pew next to Phil and my sister and brothers. It felt as if I was in a daze, and I looked up in the choir box and saw my mother looking straight at me, dabbing her eyes with a tissue, as she kept crying, almost uncontrollably. Some of the choir members were fanning her and wiping her brow. When she finally stopped crying, she looked at me and smiled. It was the first time in as long as I could remember that I saw my mother look at me lovingly. The pastor prayed. "Well, let's thank God, today, before we're dismissed, for blessing us to see what joy in him really means, by allowing us to witness his touching the heart of this child with such love and joy. Let us pray.

Oh God, we thank you for showing us, once again, that the joy of the Lord is our strength…"

And that was all I heard. By that time, I had fallen asleep on my brother, Greg's shoulder, and the next thing I knew, Phil was laying me down on my bed at home. When I saw him, I sat up, startled that he was laying me down on a bed, and thinking that he was about to begin his daily violation of my body and soul. Then, I saw Momma standing next to him. "You lay down and rest until dinner, Baby. I'll call ya' when dinner is ready." And she tenderly covered me up, after taking off my sweaty dress and under things, wiping me off, and putting my clean pajamas on me. It was so unusual for my mother to be acting in this way, because my sister, Dorothy, and I always had to help prepare dinner, set the dinner table and wash the dishes afterwards. So I just lay there, savoring the attention and lolling in the pampering I was receiving from my mother. It was heavenly.

I don't know how long I slept, maybe an hour or so—when I felt someone nudging me, saying, "C'mon now. Get up, Shelley. Go on and eat your dinner and help Dorothy clean up the kitchen. It won't be long before you need to get to bed for the night, so you can get up in the mornin' and get ready for school." Now *that* was the voice of the Gladys I *knew*, straight forward, and fairly unemotional, unless she was yelling at us kids for something. That was the voice of the mother I was *used* to. But I'll tell you what. I sure loved that voice and that Gladys who had just been so loving to me a few hours ago. I began to wonder what I could do to get her, *that* mother, to come back soon.

That was quite a unique Sunday, the Sunday I was what the people in church called "saved." It was unique because, unlike most Sundays, there was *peace* in our home. Not even Phil was being argumentative and causing everyone to be on pins and needles. He just came in from church, read the Sunday paper, looked at some baseball games on television, took a nap, and, ate dinner. It was as if he had become a different person! When I came down the stairs after Momma got me up, he said to me in a kind voice, "I made sure they saved ya' some wings, Shelley, 'cause I know that's yo' favorite part of the chicken." I was so stunned that I almost didn't know what to say. But my mother gave me a look, and I said, "Thank you." "That's OK. I was just tryin' to look out for ya'," Phil said. *What in the world has happened to him,* I wondered. *Why is he being so nice to me? What does he want?* "Listen, I'm goin' to the store to get some cigarettes, and I'll pick us up some ice cream too. Derrick, you come and ride with me so yo' momma can get some rest," Phil announced next. Derrick was always lying on or sitting up under Momma, but he got up, like Phil told him to. "Greg, you wanna' come too, and help pick out what flavor y'all want?" Phil asked. Then I knew Phil had to have taken some voodoo potion, like I'd seen in the movies, and somebody had slipped it into his food or his drink, 'cause he and Greg had barely said two words to each other since he broke Greg's arm. "OK," Greg uttered, somewhat nonchalantly. "We'll be back in a minute, Gladys," Phil advised Momma, as the three of them went out the door. I continued to eat my dinner, while Dorothy finished washing the dishes, and Momma leaned back on the couch and closed her eyes. I knew she was tired, 'cause she had worked a double shift at Drysdale's Discount Mart that Saturday. And if she was feelin' like I was, she was also exhausted from the high emotions that had filled the sanctuary at church today. So it didn't surprise me that she took this rare opportunity to close her eyes and rest. Dorothy said to me, "Ya' have to wash your own dinner plate and silverware 'cause I'm through." Her tone implied there was no negotiation on this matter. "Alright," I said. And, with that, Dorothy went upstairs and played in her room.

So I was left all alone to puzzle about Phil's sudden transformation, and to wonder if it was for real. I was still wondering that, as I was washing my dinner plate, when they returned with the ice cream. As it turned out, the decision had been to get Metropolitan flavor ice cream, so that we could each eat a little of our favorite flavor. Chocolate was my favorite, as it was Greg's. Dorothy liked vanilla, and Derrick liked strawberry. So we got out the bowls, scooped out our ice cream, and sat around the table eating so ravenously that anyone would have thought we had never had ice cream before. We joked a little, around the table, and even Phil managed a chuckle. It was so much fun that I didn't want it to come to an end, when Momma said, "OK, y'all, it's getting late. Let's clean up these dishes, and y'all go on up and get yo' baths and go to bed." "But, Momma, it's still early. Do we have to?" Derrick whined. "Yes. That goes for you *too*, Little Man, especially you 'cause you know you're the hardest to get up in the mornin,'" she said, smiling at him all the while. "And make sure y'all wash Derrick's ears good. I noticed they didn't look so clean today." And with that, the party was over. But when I went to bed that night, I dozed off to sleep still wondering, *why had this been such an awesome day? Was this some miracle? Will it last? Has Phil really changed? Are we really going to be a happy family now?*

Suffice it to say that my Heaven/Hell actuality returned with a vengeance the next day. It was harassment and abuse as usual. And that's the way it remained for far too long. The real Phil was back, as nasty and mean as he had ever been. That nice, kind Phil, who visited us yesterday, must have been a twin brother, or a long, lost cousin who just *looked* like Phil, or a figment of my imagination. In fact, in the following days it was as if that special Sunday had all been a dream. But now, I had two things that made me feel peaceful, happy, secure and loved, my lady, Jackie, and going to church every Sunday to see Mrs. Jensen and to hear about Jesus. I could hardly wait through the week for Sunday to come.

The following Sunday was a typical Sunday in our household. We went to church together, as usual. But as soon as our happy family left church, which was now my

"Shelter from the Storm," and we arrived home, the Hell that became our normal existence would be there waiting for us all. I could never figure out how Phil could be in church and act as the head of one big, happy family from the outside, and then once he got home, his mask and costume would come off, and he would resume his usual harassment, whether it was of my mother or us kids. And you know what else was strange? I knew that my *mother* truly *loved* the Lord with all of her heart. I could tell because I watched her during services, cry and praise the Lord. She just didn't have enough faith in the Lord and self-confidence to break away from Phil.

"Baby Girl, I know it's hard for ya' to understand your momma, sometimes. Am I right?" Jackie said to me one day in the bathroom after one of my daily trysts with Phil. "Jackie, why don't she fight him or leave him? Why does she let him hurt her and hurt us? Don't she love us?" I asked forlornly. "Now you shush that talk up, Little Lady. Of course your momma loves you, and you love *her*, 'cause you're family. It's just that sometimes we get so involved with life and the hardness of livin' life that we forget to love *ourselves*. Ya' see, Baby, ya' have ta' love yourself, *first*, in order to treat yourself good. Only then can ya' *truly* love someone else in a healthy manner, and express that love in the way you treat that other person. We just gotta keep prayin' that yo' momma will find the strength to love *herself* agin', enough so that she can pull herself up outta' this darkness that she's in. Your momma is in a deep, dark place, and, right now, she cain't see any light along the way. She's had a hard life and much heartache, with no one to teach her and love her through her life's difficulties. But, you mark my words, Baby Girl, one day, she's gonna' wake up and see the light that will guide her, and you children, out of this tunnel. So in the meantime, you keep on lovin' her and forgivin' her for her shortcomings, ya' hear? And you remember, Sweetheart, there is not one person on this earth who is perfect and does all the right things right every time, includin' me and you. So don't be judgin' your momma, and don't put her down, just because she's in a bad place, right now. If ya' live long enough, Baby, you'll find yourself in a bad place too, of your own making, and you'll be grateful that your family, friends, or even strangers showed you compassion. Baby Girl, I know, believe me, I know it's hard to forget the fact that yo' momma has placed you kids in this same dark place that *she's* in. And I'm not sayin' that it's right, because, even though I feel for her, I even get impatient with her for continuing to live like this. I'm not even sayin' that you should ever forget this life you're goin' through, 'cause, and you have to trust me on this, someday, your remembrance of this life will help you appreciate even *more* livin' a better life. What I am sayin', Sweetheart, is that one day you must forgive your momma, or you'll never really be free. I know it's hard right now. But, trust me, Baby Girl, one day you will have to forgive her. In the meantime, just keep on lovin' her. OK? Now I gotta' go. See ya' soon, Baby Girl."

After she left I thought about the things that my lady, Jackie had said about my momma. Although I was still angry with her for allowing us to continue to live this way, I began to hope that I *could* forgive her someday. The moments were rare when she showed real affection and love for me, but I began to realize that she probably just didn't know *how*. So I savored the moments when she *did* mother me and love me, though I never really heard her say the words, "I love you." Oh, how I longed for her to tell me that she loved me. I wondered if she ever would.

That following month, I was baptized, and, again, I felt something I hadn't felt before. Prior to being submerged in the baptism pool, however, I was scared because I didn't know how to swim. We had never taken swimming lessons, and I just knew I'd get up there and choke to death before anyone pulled me out of that water. The other thing I worried about was my hair, because Momma had just pressed and curled it the night before. What would it look like if I got it wet? Now I know that these were preposterously unfounded fears, but on *that* day, I was scared stiff. The Baptism Ministry members took me behind the baptism pool into a room and helped me take off my clothes, put on other clothes, then put on a white robe and white swim cap. I also had on white socks. I was then given instructions about how I should take a deep breath and hold it right before being submerged in the water and to cross my arms over my chest. They tried to assure me that it would be so quick there was no way I would drown, but I wasn't quite convinced. Then I heard Pastor Morris announce that we had one soul being baptized that day. The congregation began to clap, and I was led into the baptism pool, where Pastor Morris was waiting for me. Pastor Morris said some words to me, which I don't remember, because just when he was saying them, my lady Jackie, emerged from the pool, dressed in a white robe, with that big smile on her face, saying, "Baby Girl, I'm right here with you. You have nothing to fear. I'm so very proud of you, and when you come up out of that water, you're gonna' feel completely different. Trust me." And I did. I trusted her completely.

When I was submerged in that water, I could feel both Pastor Morris' and my lady Jackie's hands and arms supporting me and slowly letting me down. Then, they firmly lifted me up from the water. To my surprise, the warm water actually felt good and soothing as it cascaded over my face. I felt like I could have stayed underwater a little while longer, it felt that good! The choir was singin', *"Wade in the water, wade in the water, children, wade in the water, God's gonna' trouble the water..."* when I was being submerged, and as I came up, it sounded like their voices were the voices of angels.

After that, I was led out to dry off and put dry clothes on. All the fear that I had before, completely vanished, and, instead, I felt proud and confident that from that point on, there was someone who would always love me. I looked around for my lady, Jackie when I strutted back into the sanctuary, like a proud peacock. But I didn't see her any-more that day. After that baptism ceremony, I felt like I was the queen of the universe, and I knew that one day I would go to Heaven where I'd live with Jesus, and I would have no more pain or suffering. As my life progressed, I would come to know so much more, but for my nine-year-old heart, this was enough to make me wish I could be in church all day, every day.

Shortly thereafter, my mother befriended a white lady, named, Miss Ethel, who worked with her. She came over often and brought her four children to play with us, while she visited with my mother. Miss Ethel was in her 30's, and she was an average-sized woman, with long, bleached, strawberry blonde hair. And even though the rough texture of the skin on her face and her hands told the story of a hard road she had traveled in her life, she still always re-mained upbeat and positive. Also, she had the greatest sense of humor and brought laughter to everyone wherever she was present. Miss Ethel brought food for pitch-in din-ners most times when she came to visit. Also, she brought a cake, for dessert, each time. But this was not just any ordi-nary cake. In one of the slices of the cake, Miss Ethel placed a walnut. It became a game that whoever picked the piece of cake with the walnut in it, received a prize! We all could hardly wait for dessert to see who would win the prize! "I got it! I got it," yelled Dorothy, uncharacteristi-cally happy and enthusiastic when she picked the prize piece of cake. And, when she received the prize of two, crisp one-dollar bills, she danced around the room, waving her money in the air. Derrick, still the spoiled younger brother, folded his arms up and whined, "Why does she get everything?" The rest of us just rolled our eyes at him, since we couldn't say anything to him with our mother pre-sent.

Every time Miss Ethel came for a visit, for the first time in many years, I saw Momma laughing so hard that she said a few times, she almost wet her pants. "Girl, I told that four-eyed weasel that if he ever darkened my door again, I'd have my cousins pay him a visit so tough that he'd have to get *seven* eyes to see again, 'cause the four he has *now* wouldn't be workin'." I overheard her telling Momma one day, as they both doubled over with laughter. "What was I gonna' do with a four-eyed weasel who stayed *broke*, at that? I might even be able to overlook his crossed eyes, though they did make me dizzy half the time." My mother was almost fallin' off her chair, she was laughin' so hard. "But be broke too? Hell naw! As that ol' sayin' goes, I can do bad all by myself! Who'd he think I was – the Salvation Army? Yeah, I give to the Salvation Army, 'cause I been down and hungry myself in my lifetime, but that's different from havin' yo' man act like *you* the Salvation Army who gives him food and shelter for *free*. Now do I, in any way, resemble Mother Theresa, that saint of a woman, to you, Gladys? I'm kind, but I ain't his mother, nor the mother of any other creature in pants who claims to be a man and wants to be my man. I'm already raisin' two sons. I don't need to raise another one my own age."

My mother caught her breath long enough to say, "I'm with ya' when you're right, Ethel!" "And then this fool had the nerve to try to hit me? Girl, if my kids hadn't been there, that S.O.B would be ten feet under right now and I'd be sittin' right down there in the County Jail servin' time for killin' his miserable butt." They were laughin' so hard that it became infectious, and I started to laugh too, just because they were. We all had such a good time when Miss Ethel came over and all us kids played together like kids do. I began to see a change in Momma that I believe Miss Ethel, in particular, helped trigger. "Listen, Gladys. I really like you, and I know you're a good, hard-workin' woman. Why do you keep stayin' with this loser? Are you scared of him?" Miss Ethel asked her, one day. Yes, I usually hung around playing just close enough to them to hear what they were saying, but not so obvious that they'd make me move.

Remember, I told you that I felt older than my age. I think that's what happens to most kids whose childhood is stolen because of sexual abuse. So, naturally, I used to really enjoy listenin' to grown people talk. For some reason, I felt closer to *their* age, and *their* life's experiences than I did to kids my *own* age. "It's really hard ta' explain, Ethel. When we first met, he was really nice to me and the kids, but as soon as we moved in together, he changed. I know he's not all bad, and I guess I keep hopin' to see that same man I fell in love with come back agin," my mother said, sadly. "My God, Gladys, it's been six years, hasn't it? Do you really think he's gonna' change into Mr. Nice Guy if he hasn't done it in six years? And what about your kids? How has he treated your kids? Are they as scared of him as *you* are, Girl?" I could see Miss Ethel and Momma, ever so slightly, and I saw my mother lower her head and wipe away some tears. "Aw, Gladys, Honey, I didn't mean to hurt your feelin's. I just think you're a wonderful person who deserves so much better than him. You're still young and good lookin', Girl, and you can fall in love with a *nice* guy that's out there, who will love you for who you are, just as easily as you fell for all these losers you've had in your life. And, even more than that, suppose Mr. Right *doesn't* come along? That doesn't mean that your life is over. Ya' gotta learn to be with yourself and enjoy just bein' with yourself, Gladys. Ya' need to learn to have fun in life, and find peace with or without a man in your life. I can tell you that because it took me a long time, but I'm gettin' so much better at enjoyin' the peace of being by myself. Look, Girl, I'm gonna' start comin' to get you out of this apartment so you can hang with me and my friends. We just play cards, shoot the bull, sometimes go out for a night on the town, but we're there for each other, and we're makin' it – other women just like you and me."

Then Miss Ethel started telling my mom stories about some of the other "losers" in her own life she had encountered, in that totally hilarious way she always talked, and once again, they were both hysterical with laughter. Not long after that, Momma began to associate with other women, whom she met through Miss Ethel. These were women who were making it with their children on their own. Gradually, she seemed to be less and less involved with and concerned about Phil. As well, of late, he seemed to be home less and less, because he would stay away for days, sometimes weeks, at a time. And I began to feel like the burden of the world had been lifted from me. Then, one day, we came home, and Phil had completely moved out! What totally surprised me was that I didn't see my mother cry or become sorrowful over the fact that he was gone. In fact, there was such a peace in our home that even though we were struggling financially; we truly began to breathe again!

Chapter 4

Before long, after Phil left, we moved to the Port Charles Apartments, which were located in Eppersville Township, not too far from Randall. We had to move away from that townhouse that had brought us such grief for so many years, because my mother wanted us to start a new life in new surroundings. One night, as we were all walking up the walkway to our apartment, feeling carefree and unworried, Phil lunged from behind some bushes and began beating my mother. It was very dark outside, and he was beating my mother as if he wanted to kill her or cripple her for life. We were still just kids, and we were petrified with fear. Thank God there were neighbors who called the police. They came quickly and arrested Phil right on the spot. That was the last I saw of him for many years after that. He was finally gone. No longer were we a house full of fear. No longer did we have to put our childhood aside and be quiet so we didn't disturb the animal that lived with us. No longer were we subjected to unwarranted beatings and harassment. No longer was I the object of his sexual perversions. No longer did my older brother and sister have to witness him abusing me. No longer did my younger brother, Derrick, have to accompany him and watch him on his forays with prostitutes, while being forced to smoke marijuana with him, at the same time. Yes, he forced my little brother to do those things. No longer did my mother have to endure not only beatings and harassment, but also the shame of knowing that she had allowed this man, or *any* man, to hurt her children so gravely. He was out of our lives for good!

Miss Ethel continued to visit with her kids, and one Christmas, they surprised us by bringing us a Christmas tree. It was a white, artificial tree, and even though we had no presents, it was the most beautiful tree, and that was the most beautiful Christmas, we had spent together in years. You see, that Christmas, there was peace in our home, an environment we hadn't been in for far too many years.

Money was scarce, and we were hungry a lot, so you can imagine, I was more than happy to have dinner with a white lady, who also lived in our apartment complex. Her name was Miss Oglesby, and one day, I was jumping rope outside our apartment building when she came up to me and said. "Hi, my name is Miss Oglesby, and I live right over there in that apartment." I followed the direction her finger pointed and saw the apartment she was talking about on the first floor. "What's *your* name?" "Shelley, and we live up there," I said, pointing to our second floor apartment. Miss Oglesby was a single lady, who had no children. She was about 5 feet 5 inches tall, of average build, had light brown hair, and she wore black plastic rimmed glasses. She must have been in her 30's, and she actually reminded you of a typical school teacher. Anyway, for some reason, she took a likin' to me, and every time she saw me, she waved or greeted me, callin' out my name. "Listen. I just love to cook, but it's not as much fun when you're just cooking for yourself. Do you think your mother would mind if you had dinner with me sometime? We can also make some brownies or cookies, which ever you'd like." "Oh no," I answered quickly. "My momma won't mind at all." "Well, good, then. Why don't you come over today at about 5:00 p.m. We'll make the brownies real quick, then pop them in the oven and enjoy the aroma of them cooking while we eat our dinner. How does that sound, Shelley?" I could barely answer her, because my mind was tastin' and smellin' those chocolaty brownies! "I'll be there by 5, Miss Oglesby." "Well good, then. I'll look for you," she said with a smile in her voice. And she walked on toward her apartment. I almost couldn't contain myself I was so happy.

That evening, I kept looking at the clock. For some reason, time seemed to go by extremely slowly. I had bathed and put on clean clothes and was ready almost two hours before it was time to go to dinner. So, when the time came, I ran over to her apartment like a gazelle. I knocked on her door, and when she opened it, she greeted me with a big hug. "Come on in, Shelley, and make yourself at home. Come on back to the kitchen and help me finish up." And that's how I began having dinners with Miss Oglesby. In fact, we began having dinner together several times a week. Momma was usually working, and it certainly didn't matter to my brothers and sisters that I was having dinner with this nice lady, Miss Oglesby, because it really meant there would be more food at home for *them*. Her table was set with a beautiful, white tablecloth and napkins, silverware that sparkled, and two wine glasses, one for her, and one for me, at each of our meals. I always drank juice, and it made me feel very grown-up to sip my juice from a wine glass. I'm not sure, but I think she drank wine from hers.

The food usually tasted very good, and I devoured it. But, on this particular night, she had cooked brussel sprouts, which I didn't like at all. It was all I could do to swallow them, I disliked them so much. After we had eaten, she told me to come with her to her bedroom. I didn't think anything about that, because, I had been coming to her apartment and having dinner with her for about a month, and she had always been so kind to me. When I walked in her bedroom, she told me to have a seat on the

58

And Yet, You Still Chose Me

floor. Being a child, I didn't think sitting on the floor was an unusual request, because at home, and at school, we did it all the time. Then, out of no where, she suddenly lifted my skirt, located my panties, and pulled my panties off. I became very frightened and confused, when that happened; but I still couldn't imagine that she would do anything to harm me. Then she told me to open my legs. "Why?" I asked, since my radar was on full alert by now. "Oh, don't be scared, Shelley. I won't hurt you. We're friends, right?" she asked convincingly. "Yeah," I answered, somewhat cautiously. "Well, friends trust each other, and would never hurt each other. So I'm not going to hurt you, Shelley. I've really grown very fond of you, and I want to get closer to you. OK? Now, just open your legs for me as wide as you can." I did what she said. Then she took a pencil and slowly started pushing it up in my womanhood, as far as she could. I started to cry from the pain, which was especially extreme since I was still sitting upright on the floor, not lying down. I guess my crying brought her back to her senses, because she removed the pencil, quickly. I jumped up, grabbed my panties, and bolted out that door. "Shelley, Shelley. Please don't go. I'm sorry if I hurt you. Please don't go," she yelled after me, in a voice filled with alarm and panic. But she couldn't catch me.

When I got to our apartment, no one was home; and I was grateful for that. I was grateful that I could, once again, cry my tears without anyone ever knowing that I had done so. Of course, I never told a soul in my home what had happened. I was too ashamed and hurt. "Baby Girl, are you bleedin'? Let me take a look at ya'. I saw what happened, and I'm so mad at that hussy, I started to come and throw her out that window, drag her to the dumpster and throw her in! But I'm not here to do that." Jackie asserted, as angry as I'd ever seen her. Then she opened her huge purse and got out that wonderful white towel, a matching face cloth, that wonderful bottle of lotion, and another tiny bottle of something that looked like oil. After she bathed me,

(Yes, we were in the bathroom, as usual.), she said, "Here, Baby Girl, I'm gonna' give you this bottle of healing oil, and I want you to put some on your finger and put it up as high as you can where that pencil went. OK?" Following her instructions, I put the oil on my finger and put it in my womanhood where the pencil had entered. Almost immediately, I felt a cool, soothing feeling, and the pain and irritation I had been feeling disappeared. "It feels good. But, you know what? It feels icky and strange up in me. Is that the way it's supposed to feel?" I asked. Slightly amused, she said, smiling, "Well, Baby Girl, I guess by your asking me that question, it's time for you to get the right information and truth about the make-up of your body. So, I'll start teachin' ya' what ya' need to know, when ya' need to know it. OK? We'll start right now." And with that, my lady Jackie started educating me, at the level my mind could take it in, about the human body, my body, in particular. It was the first of many lessons to come, but what I was most grateful for was her patience in answering my questions, as well as, her refusal to talk down to me, as if I had not experienced sexual encounters in my life, albeit, in the most horrific manner.

Needless, to say, I never saw Miss Oglesby again, nor did she try to contact me. In fact, I think she moved out of the complex a day or two after that pencil incident. I was glad, because I never wanted to see her again. Looking at this young woman, who appeared to be a professional person, with a good background and a kind heart, who would have imagined that she would turn out to be such a tortured soul? I certainly would never have believed it, nor did I think anyone else would. As I reflect on it, *now*, it almost seemed as if she was *courting* me; because the food was usually exquisite, the table was set beautifully, and the atmosphere was really romantic. I truly believe she had a romantic interest in me, now that I look back on it. So, as a consequence of that encounter, my guard went back up, again, and I felt I would never trust another adult in my life, except my lady, Jackie, nor would I be fooled again by outward expressions of kindness. Never again!

Never say never!

Though my mother worked hard, trying to take care of us and pay the bills, she just couldn't keep up with the expenses. We were truly poor, and the kids in the neighborhood teased us unmercifully. They said horrible, hurting things, like, "Y'all so poor, you have to keep dead bodies in the freezer to have somethin' to eat for dinner." Where does that kind of cruelty come from in children? Do they learn it from their parents? Or, probably more the case, do they just want to go along with the leader of the pack and be how he or she is to fit in? Well, that's a whole other story, about peer pressure to conform, which I won't delve into here.

One Tuesday, we came home from school and found all of our belongings strewn out on the ground, because we had been evicted from our apartment. Momma had no money to pay the rent, so our only alternative was to be housed by the state, which put us up in a motel in a nearby town. That motel became our home, for a time, and there were other state-sponsored tenants at that same motel. Eventually, my mother brought a new male friend, Clarence Eaton, to the place we called home at the motel. Clarence was tall and skinny (she seemed to be attracted to tall, skinny men), and he wore his hair in an Afro. Clarence "stayed clean," as we used to say, because he always dressed very well. He also drove a bright, red Volkswagen, which we loved. Clarence treated us well, and he was a kind man. He brought us food and snacks all the time, and, occasionally, he'd sleep over on the sofa, but he did not live with us. Clarence was not a "church-going" man, so my mother sent us kids to a community church on the bus with the other children who stayed at the motel. She usually stayed behind with him at the motel, while we were at church. Furthermore, I never heard Clarence expressing any *desire* to go to church with us. I often wondered, however, why Momma stopped going, just because *he* didn't go. I believe that was a mistake, on her part, because, at one time, she really *loved* the Lord. In every other way, however, Clarence was nicer to us than any other man had ever been, and we were all happy just because we didn't have to be around *Phil* any longer.

On this particular Sunday when we returned from church, Clarence was still there. I was almost ten years old, at that time, and I had just begun to feel safe and free, again. I still felt so happy in church, but now I also felt happy coming home from church, with all the other children. Each Sunday, we ran off the church bus, ready to play outside. I could not wait to play outside! When we opened the door to the motel room, Clarence asked my mother if he could take me to the store around the corner to get ice cream for all the children. (Ice cream was still the Sunday treat all us kids craved the most.) Momma looked down at me, with a blank stare, smiled at Clarence, and said yes. I skipped to his car, and we drove off to the store around the corner. When we got there, he let me get any ice cream I wanted. I was so excited, and I got my favorite Orange Dreamcicle. I began sucking on that Orange Dreamcicle, and it tasted so good.

We got in the car and drove off, but, suddenly, he slowed the car down. I could feel my heart begin to beat faster, and thought it was pounding so loud that even Clarence could hear it. This feeling was all too familiar to me, because it was the rapid heartbeat that accompanied fear and anxiety. Then the car came to a complete stop, and he began to tell me how pretty I was. Without warning, he reached over for me, and before I knew it, he put his tongue practically down my throat. Ice cream was dripping everywhere in his car, and some got on my clothes. The memories from the previous years, with Phil, started flooding back, and I started pushing him away, not willing to just let him have his way with me. No! Not this time, my soul seemed to cry out! But then, just as suddenly as he started it, Clarence stopped "tonguing" me, and we drove home. I got out of the car, as if nothing had happened, which is what I had always done, and ran upstairs to the bathroom. I snatched off my clothes, and began scrubbing my face. Then I brushed my teeth so hard my gums started bleeding.

"Here, Baby Girl. Wash your mouth out with this." My lady, Jackie handed me a small bottle with a purple-colored liquid in it. I rinsed my mouth repeatedly with it until all the liquid was gone. Like everything else she gave me, it made my mouth feel cleaner than I'd ever felt before. "I know you must have some questions after that fool put his tongue down your throat. Don't ya'? Well, you know you can ask me. Now, c'mon. Ask me, Baby Girl." "Jackie, what was he doing? Why did he put his tongue in my mouth? Is that the way you kiss somebody? I've seen some of that in the movies and on TV, but it felt like I was chokin,' and his breath smelled so *bad*. Is that what grown people do, and do they really *like* it?" She was so tickled, she could barely keep from laughing, but she cleared her throat and said, "Sweetheart, no one should have to put up with bad breath, and when you're older and datin', you make sure you keep that in your mind. Do not date anyone with bad breath, 'cause if they're not clean enough to keep their teeth and breath clean, then who knows what else they don't keep clean? That's what you call triflin', and you don't need to be around anyone that's triflin'. Now, as for your other questions about whether or not grown people kiss like that, let me just say that when they do, it should be pleasurable and enjoyable to both people. In other words, Suga', they're not chokin' each other, like you just experienced. How can a person enjoy the kiss if they feel like they chokin'? No, Honey. It's not supposed to be like that. If the two people really love and have deep feelings for one another, they will want to give that other person pleasure, not pain, and they certainly won't want to choke them to death. You'll see, one day, Little Lady, and you'll know the difference. Trust me. Now, Baby Girl, I'm gonna' say somethin' to you today that I want you to never, ever forget. Your life has been filled with so much hurt and pain and abuse that it's a wonder you don't just crawl in a corner somewhere and never come out. But look at ya'. You're still standin' and breathin' and curious about life. And, you're still lookin' for Jesus. Now, I don't know why people keep usin' and abusin' you, Sweetheart, but I *do* know that you've gotta' stay strong through it all, because one day, you're gonna' look back on this life and understand why all this happened to *you*. I know there is something important for you to do in your life, and you've gotta' keep on goin' and lookin' for Jesus no matter what's happenin' in your life right now. Trouble don't last always, Suga', and I promise you, one day you'll see that. Trust me." Then she held me close for a long time, rocking me back and forth, as she always did. And I felt comforted by her, as I always did. After that, Clarence still came around for a short time, and then he moved on. He never touched me again, nor was I ever alone with him again. I made sure of that!

There was a large farm located behind the motel. A few of us kids would go to the farmhouse, and the owner allowed us to ride on his horses and feed his chickens. We had so much fun! He showed us his barn house where he housed all the pigs, and I began to notice that when he stood behind me to point out the different kinds of pigs, he pressed hard against me. He also raised my shirt and placed his wrinkled, white hands on my breasts. I didn't protest, because I thought this is what men *did* to little girls, and he also did the same thing to the other girls in the group. We all just put our hands over our mouths and started gigglin' when he did that, and we didn't think anything of it.

"Why do you keep lettin' that ol' fart do that to you, Shelley MacDonald? Haven't you learned anything from me?" It was my lady, Jackie, and, for the first time ever, I really thought she was mad at me. "It didn't hurt, Jackie. And he might not let me come back and play here if I don't let him do that. We were in the barn, and I was brushing one of the horses." "Ya' know what? I think I've been givin' you too much credit. I thought you had more sense and self-pride than you're showin' me here. Don't you know that if it takes a man or boy touchin' ya' anywhere on your body for him to give ya' what you want in return, then you don't *need* whatever it is he's givin' ya'? Shelley, and that's what I'm gonna' call ya' from now on, instead of Baby Girl, because you're certainly not a baby, and I'm not gonna' baby ya' anymore. Remember when we talked about how your momma needed to begin lovin' herself agin' so she would stop allowin' herself to be misused, oppressed and abused by anyone? Well, Young Lady, you'd better start takin' a good look at *yourself*! Because if you start rationalizin' and lettin' men *use* you, and use your body, so they'll let you have what you want, then you'll end up in the same dark place your mother's been in. Do you know what a prostitute is, Shelley? Or some people even call them whores or ho's? "I think so," I said. "Well, prostitutes are girls or women, and sometimes boys or men, who usually let people have sex with them for money, drugs or somethin' they want, kinda' like you're lettin' that ol' farmer feel on your body so you can keep comin' here to play on his farm. Whores, or ho's, as you kids call them, may or may not receive anything in return for sex. They're just known to be "easy," when it comes to havin' sex, 'cause they don't seem to care who they have it with. Now, I'm not judgin' people who do that, 'cause everybody has their own life story and reasons why they do things in life. And I never want you to judge them, either. All I'm tryin' to show you is that if you want a better life than you're livin' now, you're gonna' have to start respectin' yourself and your body in order to make others respect you, Shelley, whether it's an adult or a child. You deserve to be treated well and with respect, Shelley MacDonald, and don't you ever forget that! But you gotta show that you have respect for *yourself*. Listen, Suga'. Like I been teachin' ya', this human body of ours is a miraculous creation by God. We have to take good care of it, because it is also the house that our souls and spirits live in. I know you heard in church that our bodies are the temples of the soul. Right? I nodded in agreement. "Well, what that means is that we've gotta' take as good care of our bodies, and have as much respect and reverence for them as we have for the church building, or temple, where we worship. You wouldn't do anything bad to your church would you? You wouldn't let anyone just come in the church and use it to have drinkin' parties, sex parties, and drug parties in, would you? Well, in that same way, you cannot let anyone use your body, or you yourself use your body for anything that would disgrace it, abuse it, or dishonor it in any way. I'm talkin' to you this way, Shelley, because you're getting' older, and you need to understand that you've gotta' make some choices and decisions about who you want to be, and how you want to live. I know that you're still young, Suga', and everything about your life isn't all under your control right now. But some things are. So, you need to start makin' choices that help you have a better life. OK? Well, I know that may be a lot for you to understand right now, but I also know that you've got some wisdom in ya' beyond yo' years. Ya' just need to use it. Now, you find some other place to play and enjoy yourself, and never come back to this farm again! Ya' hear me?" "Yes, ma'am," I said, almost in tears. "And dry up those tears, 'cause they won't work on me today. You go home and think about all the conversations we've had about who ya' are, whose ya' are, and what ya' deserve to look for in life. And when I see ya' again, I want ya' to tell me who ya' are, and what ya' want and expect in life. Alright? A part of getting' what ya' want, Sweetheart, is you carryin' yo'self in a way that seems like you've already got it. I'll explain that to ya' later. Now give me a hug and get on home." I never wanted Jackie to be angry or disappointed in me again. It made my heart sink at the thought of losing her from my life. *What would I do if I didn't have Jackie?*

After that, I no longer looked at going to the farm and playing in the barn in the same way. I stopped going there, because, even though I didn't fully understand what Jackie had told me, I did know that I didn't want men or boys to think I was some ho' that they could just use anytime they wanted to anymore. I had had enough of that! And I never went back to that farm, again, even though it meant missing some fun with the other kids. I guess I really was trying to be a better person, and was reaching for a better life, even if I couldn't articulate what that meant at that time.

Just like every other place we had lived, our time was up at the motel, and we had to move on. Everyone who lived in the motel received funding from the state. It was, actually, more like a shelter, because everyone in the motel had no other place to go. Momma tried her best to make ends meet, with the little money she made, combined with the limited knowledge she had of raising children on her own. But she struggled with the weight of the responsibility. So, when we had to move from the motel, we moved back to Randall and stayed with a friend of Momma's, Miss Angela. Miss Angela didn't try to hide the fact that she really didn't want us in her house. But can you blame her? Who would want your house suddenly invaded by four kids and their mother? She also had a son of her own, and he was very spoiled. Miss Angela worked at a gum factory, and when she came home from work, she brought with her all kinds of bubble gum and candy, and gave it to all us kids. But, still she constantly looked at us as if we were just in her way. In the beginning, I certainly didn't feel welcomed there.

Miss Angela was a sharp dresser, and when she and Momma prepared to go out partying for the night, she got clean. Her clothes always looked good on her, and she had practically every closet in her house filled with her clothes. Mother and Miss Angela started going out "clubbin'" several nights a week. So, at least Momma seemed to be havin' a good time with Miss Angela. Loud music was playing all the time, in her house, and despite Miss Angela's attitude toward us kids, we found a way to be happy, and it was the first time I felt I was at home, with no men around to abuse me. One day, Miss Angela and my mother were in the kitchen, and I was curious to see what they were doing, because they seemed so happy. They were dancin' and drinkin', and, as I walked around the corner, I noticed a round mirror on the table with white lines of powder on it. I thought it was baby powder, at first. Then I looked over at Miss Angela's hands, and saw that she was holding a small, brown bottle, no bigger than my pinky finger. There was also a small spoon that she was repeatedly dipping from the bottle to her nose. Next, she placed the white powder on the mirror in small, straight lines and reached over for one of the smallest straws I had ever seen. She sniffed the powder up her nose through that tiny straw. Then she gave some to my mother. I didn't understand what they were doing, but I did know something did not seem right. As my lady Jackie had said, I did have awareness and wisdom beyond my age, and I was very curious from the day my innocence was stripped away from me.

Over the next few months, Miss Angela's house became the party house on the block. All the kids in the neighborhood would hang out there. Even kids who were much too old to come there, set up camp with us younger children, who lived there. My mother and Miss Angela were using drugs all the time, now, and were always so high, they didn't realize what was going on in the house. And that's how I met the young man who became the first person I fell in love with. He was a part of the crew who hung out at the house, sometimes until dawn. I was only 11 years old, at that time, and he was 17. I don't know how he ended up practically living in our home, but he did. His name was Jerome.

My mother continued to work every day, even though she got high at night. She was such a hard worker. One day, I remember her walking through the door looking so sad. I jumped up off Jerome's lap and asked, "What's the matter, Momma?" She answered, "I was just fired from my job." She was so devastated. Despair was written all over her face, and her body was slumped like a prize fighter who was about to be knocked out. From that time on, she sank deeper into her drug habit. Even before my mother lost her job, however, the house was completely out of control. Let me describe our home then. It stayed full of both adults using crack cocaine and teenagers to young adults smoking marijuana. I know you've seen that in movies or on television, but I actually *lived* it! It is truly amazing that neither I, nor my sister, nor my brothers got hooked on drugs, at that time, even though our home became the neighborhood drug/party house. We had lived there for several months, when Miss Angela suddenly packed up, and she and her son moved out. As we found out later, she was being evicted so she cleared the house of all of her belongings and left. Not too long afterward, Miss Angela ended up being arrested and going to prison. I understand it had something to do with her trying to feed her drug addiction. In the meantime, we stayed on there, because we had no money and no where else to go. Miss Angela moved all of her furniture out, so that meant we ended up sleeping on the floor, for the most part. The house became inundated with people of all ages, and none of the best character. We, kids, were virtually raising ourselves. My older brother, Greg, began to have a lot of parties, and some guys who lived in the adjacent housing sub-divisions were his DJs. They were well known DJs all over the city of Randall.

Jerome Washington, my first love, was one of the DJs. He was 17 years old, an *older* man, and I was enamored with him from the first time I saw him. He was about six feet tall, with neatly braided corn rows, and a hefty football player's physique. I thought he was s-o-o-o fine! When they came to our house to DJ my brother's party one night, they never really left. Our house became the "hot spot" for many, frequent neighborhood parties. In fact, everyone at school and in the neighborhood knew that our house was the place to be for parties every weekend. As young as I was, I still partied with the older kids. Jerome kept looking at me all through that first party. Then, he came over to me and said, "Your hair is so beautiful, Brown Suga.'" I giggled, not mature enough to know how to respond to a compliment from an older man.

The party got pretty loud and raucous, and when some of the guys started using profanity, I heard Jerome say to them, "Yo' man. Watch your mouth! My girl's around." *He called me his girl*, I thought about to jump up and down with excitement. I had butterflies in my stomach just thinking about him. And that's the way he began to become my "protector," who cared about me so much that he wouldn't let anything happen to me. "Come here, Brown Suga'." And when I walked over to him, he held me, caressed me, and had me sit on his lap. I thought he was wonderful, and I began to fall in love, or so I thought. So the whole DJ crew began to live there, as many others did.

Then I heard her. "You'd better watch yourself, Young Lady, before you step into somethin' you'll be sorry about later." It was my lady, Jackie, and she had kept me going all through seeing my mother slide deeper into her addiction, seeing my home become a drug haven and seeing what childhood I had left, virtually disappear. I might have been on drugs, myself, if it hadn't been for her. But this one time, I didn't want to listen to Jackie. "Shelley, you've never really seen real, true and righteous love between a man and a woman, so this thing you're feelin' right now, it's what's called lust, Baby, not love. Yeah, he's cute, alright, but being cute doesn't mean he's right, Shelley, Girl. But you know what, I know you're smellin' yourself. What I mean by that is, I know you think you're a woman now, because you've had more experience than girls your age should ever have, but you're not a woman until you can think and make decisions like a woman—like a woman who respects and loves herself. You know I've always told you the truth, don't you? But, I also know that this time, unlike before, you're probably not goin' to listen to me, are you? OK, Missy, I think, even though I love you, I'm gonna' have to let you find out for yourself the hard way. Now, I'm not sayin' that I won't be here for you. You know I love you too much for that. But I'll just wait for you to call on me. Do you understand? Now give me my hug. I love you very much, Shelley. Be careful, Suga'." And she was gone.

After I had showered one day, I was coming out of the bathroom, with my towel wrapped around me, and Jerome was walking my way in the hallway. He said to me, "I dare you to drop that towel." Wanting to appear grown up and unafraid, I took the dare and dropped the towel. Jerome stared at my body, with his eyes going from my head to my feet. I quickly grabbed the towel up and covered myself. "I dare you to do it again," Jerome prodded me. Without hesitation, I dropped the towel again. Then he walked over to me, fondled my breasts, as if he was in awe of them, and uttered, "Uh-uh-uh! Brown Suga', you gotta' body that makes a man wanna' holla'! Can I kiss you?" "Sure," I said, trying to appear confident and womanly. Then he turned my chin to face him, leaned down, and gave me a long, slow, lingering kiss. Next, he kissed my neck, ever so sweetly. By that time, I was swooning, and I wanted every bit of him, like he wanted me. He led me to my bedroom, and laid me on the floor. "Is this your first time?" he asked. "Yes," I answered quickly, in some way knowing that's what he wanted to hear. When he entered my womanhood, I jerked because I remembered the pain that Phil had caused me. But, within a few minutes it felt like, somehow, this was different. He gradually moved inside me, checking, periodically, to see if I was OK. What had been so painful with Phil, the monster, seemed to be almost enjoyable with Jerome, because we were really making love, not just having sex. At least that's what Jerome called it. The more I relaxed, the more pleasurable it became. It just seemed right, because I was Jerome's girl, and we loved each other. Jackie didn't really understand, though we hadn't talked since that last visit when she warned me about Jerome. I knew that Jerome was right for me, and she was wrong! I knew that loving Jerome was the right decision for me, and not even Jackie, as wonderful and wise as she was, was right *all* the time, I persuaded myself. Thus began my four-year relationship with my older man, Jerome. I'll tell you more about Jerome and me a little later.

Money became almost non-existent, after Momma lost her job at Drysdale's Discount Mart. This meant Momma had to figure out how we could even eat. Catsup, mayonnaise and blue cheese dressing sandwiches, with an ice cold drink of sugar water (not to be mistaken for Kool-Aid) became our daily fare, just to keep from being hungry. We didn't even think about complaining. Our luxury dinner was good ol' onion rings, prepared in our special way. We cut up the raw onions, seasoned them with salt and pepper, floured the onions, and deep fried them in recycled oil. (This was cooking oil we re-used because we couldn't afford to buy fresh oil – not because we were conservationists!) We didn't even miss the fact that there was no batter for the onion rings, since all we had was flour. This was our fine dining, at the time. Eventually, however, Momma had to make some tough decisions, and she decided to split up the family, because she could no longer afford to take care of us.

So Dorothy, my sister, went to Illinois to stay with Momma's cousin, Rachael. Then, out of desperation, she tracked down our father, and decided to send my older brother, Greg, and me to Detroit, Michigan to visit him. I did not know my father, nor did I have a desire to know him, at that time, because I thought I was a woman in love, and I didn't want to leave my man, even for a short visit. I was not a happy camper about this visit.

Chapter 5

When Momma explained to Greg and me that we were go-ing to Detroit, Michigan just for a short visit, even though I still preferred to stay in Randall with Jerome, I resigned myself to making the trip, and just wanted to hurry up and get it over so I could get back to my lover, my man, Jerome. Another reason I didn't want to be away was be-cause my younger brother, Derrick, and I had become very attached. I took on the role of being a mother to him, be-cause our mother was not able to care for him, as she had before. It was *me* that little Derrick clung to now, and it seemed natural to me to look after him. He no longer was the whiney "thorn in our side" that he *had* been, after he realized that he needed us to survive. Derrick wasn't going on the trip to Detroit with us, so I just wanted to make the trip and get it over with. There was no way I was going to be apart from my baby brother for very long, either, just as I wasn't going to be separated from my Jerome!

So off we went, me, Greg and Momma on our Grey-hound bus trip to Detroit. It was an extremely long trip, and I swore I'd never make that trip again.

Every seat on the bus was taken. I don't know how many babies there were, but they all seemed to be crying at the same time. There was a horrible stench on the bus, because the toilet would not flush, and it was overflowing. I soon learned that on long rides, like this one, it is hard to contain what your body needs to do naturally. It was especially hard for the man sitting in the seat next to my brother, Greg. He was sitting in front of me and Momma, when, out of nowhere, there was a familiar sound that each and every one of us knows. It was the sound of someone passing gas (or farting, as some people describe it). The smell of rotten eggs filled the cabin of that bus almost immediately. My brother, Greg, looked back at us, with his hand over his nose and mouth, pointing to the man sitting next to him. I started laughing, hysterically. I just couldn't help it. Momma, who was laughing, too, behind the hand she had placed over her nose and mouth, said, "Sh-sh-sh! Both of you. Before that man gets mad!" Then I looked around, and everyone on the bus had their hands over their noses, trying to drown out that horrid smell! On top of all this, the air conditioning system suddenly decided not to work. It was truly Murphy's Law – everything that could go wrong, *did* go wrong.

My dad, Henry, was there to greet us at the bus station when we finally arrived in Detroit. I was slightly distant, at first, because I really didn't know this man, plus, even though I couldn't put my finger on the reason why, I sensed something was just not right about all of this. But my brother and I were both so exhausted that I couldn't dwell on whatever was making me feel uneasy. I just wanted to lay my head down and sleep. "So how you kids doin'," my dad asked. "OK," I answered, shrugging my shoulders in a detached manner. "How was the trip comin' here," he said. "Long," I said, rubbing my eyes. Tiring," Greg answered. "Well, let's get you home," he added. Home? In my mind I questioned his use of the term, because this was *not* my home. There was a kind of awkwardness to our attempts at conversation, because he didn't really know *us*, and we really didn't know *him*. As we drove through the city of

Detroit, I noticed there were many big buildings. But I also noticed a lot of people walking the streets, and I thought, *I wonder why they all look so scary?* It was about 3:00 a.m., and while I didn't realize it then, I now know that these people were chasing the midnight high that they had earlier, and wanted again. My dad drove down a dark street, pulled up in front of a house, and dropped my mother off, to our great surprise! "Y'all stay with your daddy tonight, and I'll see y'all in the mornin'," she explained. And we drove off. "Whose house is that," I asked. "It's your mom's Cousin Joyce's house. You probably don't remember her," my dad explained.

The moment we got to my dad's apartment, I knew I did not want to be there. He lived in an area of Detroit called Death Valley. This area of the city was given this name by the police, because of the number of shootings and murders that took place there, and the name had caught on in the community, as well. When we went into the apartment, my dad introduced us to his wife, Geraldine, and her son, Marlin. There were also four or five people sitting at a table playing cards. I don't remember all of their names. Geraldine smiled at us, as she smoked a cigarette with one hand on her hip. As she smiled, I watched the cigarette smoke make its way through a space where a tooth should have been in her mouth. Me and Greg just looked at each other, trying very hard not to laugh out loud. Marlin was tall and sinewy, like a basketball player. He was 15 years old. "Are y'all hungry?" Geraldine asked. "No ma'am," we both answered truthfully, because we were too tired and sleepy to eat. "Well, y'all must be plain exhausted from that long bus ride, so let me just show you where you're gonna' sleep." As it turned out, we didn't have to go far, because my bed was actually the sofa, and my brother had to sleep on the floor. I was so tired I was almost numb, and I laid down on that sofa and went to sleep almost immediately.

The sound of music playing, voices cursin' and yellin', and the smell of alcohol filling the air, woke me up out of my sleep. As I started opening my eyes, I was still so sleepy and groggy that I couldn't quite remember where I was. I felt so confused, at first. Then, I turned my face toward the back of the sofa. As my eyes slowly opened, and I looked up; there was a large cockroach crawling along the top of the sofa. That woke me up in a hurry, and I was no longer confused about where I was. I quickly plucked that cockroach off the sofa with my finger, and no one even noticed me doing it. My father's apartment was not very big, so every word that was spoken could be heard from every room. My brother, Greg, was still lying on the floor, deep in sleep. He must have been so wiped out that even the noise in the apartment didn't awaken him. So I continued to lie there, on the sofa, and I drifted off to sleep again until the next morning.

As I covered my face with the dingy, stained blanket they had given me, I suddenly heard loud noises - ...Pop...Pop...Pop...Pop... *Was this a car backfiring, or could it really be gunshots?* My mind was racing with fear. I had never really heard gunshots before, except in movies or on TV. My brother jumped up, and everyone at the table ducked and started to scatter. I didn't know what to think or do. My dad started screaming, "Lay down on the floor! Get down! Get down!" Greg immediately grabbed me and pulled me down on the floor, covering my body with his. As it turned out, there was a man in front of our complex with a machine gun who was shooting at anyone who came across his path. It seemed like an eternity, because I was so scared, but after only a short time, I heard sirens, and the gunshots suddenly ceased. I peeked out the window, and saw several policemen with their guns drawn, pointing toward the man. It was as if I were looking at a movie. Ambulances were everywhere. I watched them haul the shooter out of the complex like a rag doll. He was a tall, skinny, black man with an Afro. He had no shirt, socks or shoes on.

He only wore a pair of jeans. Boy was I scared! Then, I began to hear the birds start to chirp outside, as the sun began to rise, just as if nothing had happened.

I sat back down on the sofa, trying to grasp what just took place. Some of the people who were in the apartment just stood there, while others just sat still. It was so quiet that you could hear everyone breathing heavily in the room. We were all in a state of shock. I didn't know what to think or what to say. When I finally opened my mouth, I said, "Dad where is my mother? I want to go home." He just stood there and stared at me, with a blank look on his face. So, thinking he hadn't heard me, I repeated myself, "Dad, I want to go home. Please call Momma." As he stood there looking down at me, I could see that there was no mistake he was the father of my older brother and me. Both of us looked just like him. He was about 5 feet, 9 inches tall and weighed about 185 pounds. His skin was a golden brown color, and his hair was thick and curly. I also had his slanted eyes. I mentioned that his hair was curly, but the curliness was the result of his having a "Jeri Curl." As a matter of fact, as time went on, a great many black folks had "Jeri Curls," including me, during that time. Then, I began to smell the stench of alcohol pervading the entire apartment, and I could tell that my dad was totally drunk. He continued to look at me with that blank stare of intoxication, so I reached up and tugged on his green pants. Mind you, these were not just *any* green pants. These were bright, lime green pants, and I could tell that my dad really thought he was stylin' in those lime green pants, with his thick-soled black shoes. So again, tugging gently on his pants, I said, "Dad, please call Momma to come and get us. I want to go home!"

Everyone in the room suddenly looked at me, including Greg. Then my father finally said these words that changed my entire life forever, "You ain't never goin' home 'cause your momma's gonna' put you up for adoption if you go back." I could not believe what he was telling me. My mind was racing a million miles a minute. I looked at him, again. Then I looked over at my brother, and the expression on my face said to him, "What's he talking about? Why is he lying to me?" My big brother, Greg, just stood there quietly. He never was a trouble-maker. But I believe he already *knew*, because he just looked the other way. I screamed. "No! No! No! I want my mother," I yelled at the top of my voice, as tears gushed down my face. My dad then told me she had already gone back home to Maryland, and that she had left early that morning.

For several days, after that, I just felt sick, and I did not, *could not*, eat. I was devastated and kept asking over and over in my mind, *How could she have done this to us? Why? I had made such an effort of trying to stay out of her way, but, now, she didn't even want me near her?* Even with all that I had been through in my short life up 'til then, that day was one of the lowest days in my life. I was almost thirteen years old, and I just wanted to die. I felt so depressed. My father, lacking *any* trace of sensitivity, then told me, "Ya' better get yourself together, Shelley, 'cause you're not goin' back. You're gonna' live here with us, and stop worryin' about that little thug back there, too. What's his name? Jerome? You ain't ever gonna' see him again," he said sternly. "Yeah, your momma told me all about him, and how fast you've gotten since you started foolin' around with him. He's way too old for you, and we could really put him in jail for messin' with you at your age. But we both agreed, your momma and me, that the best thing to do was to get you away from him" Under my breath, I was saying, *Who are you? You don't even know me, and Momma can't even make decisions for herself, let alone for me!* "So settle yourself down and make yourself comfortable here. This is your home now," he said Immediately, I resolved, *That's what <u>you</u> think! I'm gettin' out of here as soon as I can!*

"Well, well, well, Shelley, Girl! What have you gotten yourself into now? No, I shouldn't say that, 'cause your momma really brought you here. I know you're thinkin'

about gettin' out of here as soon as you can. But you need
to slow down, Shelley. Just slow your roll. I can understand
why you wanna' get away from here. In some ways, it's as
bad, or even *worse*, than where you *were*, with all this
shootin' and killin' madness. Believe me, I would rather
you weren't here. But where are you thinkin' about goin' if
you leave here?" Jackie asked. "I'm gonna' find Momma,
Derrick, and Jerome," I said with complete confidence.
"So, you don't believe what your dad said about your
momma not wantin' you?" "He's just lyin'. I just think she
might be broke, and didn't know how she would take care
of all of us. But I don't believe she don't want us," I declared. "I see. Well, if that is the case, how will your goin'
back change that situation? Do you have some money to
help her out?" "Not right now. But I'll find a way! I know I
will!" "Yeah, I'm sure you will. But will it be the right
way? That's my big question for you, Shelley. You know,
Baby. I said I wasn't gonna' call you Baby no more, but
you still my Baby. I've been watchin' you, 'cause I'm always with you, even when you don't see me. And because I
love you, I've been troubled by how you've been livin'
your life, Shelley. Remember when we were on the farm,
and we talked about how you should never let anyone just
use your body for their own pleasure, just so you can get
something that you want? Do you remember that?" "Yeah,"
I said, almost inaudibly. "Then why are you lettin' this
Jerome character treat you like you was a piece a' meat,
Shelley? Have you completely turned away from all that
you've been taught in church, and by me, about right
livin'? Have you completely lost touch with the foundation
that has carried you through your very difficult life up to
this point? Where is the Shelley that loved Jesus and loved
His church? I'm askin' because I don't know this *new* Shelley."

Whereupon, I burst out in tears, gaspin', "But Jackie,
you don't understand. Jerome is the only man that has ever
really *loved* me! I know he's rough with me, sometimes,

and he drinks a lot, but he would never really hurt me or leave me. I *know* it! And, Jackie, if you been seein' me, then you know we been so poor, sometimes we hardly have anything to eat. And Momma? Well, Momma just stays high all the time, tryin' not to face how we all livin'. Jackie, Jesus don't seem to care about us, right now. If He *did*, why would He 'cause all this to happen to us? You said He's in control of everything," I said, seeking answers. "Now wait a minute, Shelley," Jackie said, with her hand on her hip. "You know better than that. You know that Jesus doesn't 'cause bad things to happen to us. But if He *allows* those things to happen, you must know and believe that He has a greater plan for you. That's how you make it through these hard times, Shelley. You gotta' believe and know that it ain't gonna' be like this always. And that you're gonna' have a better life. I know that's hard to do, Baby. Don't get me wrong. I wish you weren't goin' through these troubles. But I know you are destined for greater things, Shelley. Trust me. You *are*! But you growin' up now, much faster than most, I'm sorry to say. So you gotta' make your own decisions and live with the consequences of those decisions, Shelley. I just pray most of them will be good decisions for you. But no matter, I'm always here for you, because I love you. Now c'mon here and give me my hug," Jackie said, crying softly. Then she was gone.

The next morning, my dad and Geraldine went to work. They both worked in housekeeping at the Days Inn Motel. In fact, that's where they met. It was a Friday. And, as I came to know, like every Friday, it was Poker and Black Jack night at the MacDonald's place. There was plenty of Colt 45, Old English, and Thunderbird, which good ol' Mr. Russell, who was a friend of Dad's, always brought. Mr. Russell was in his 50's, wore tons of chains around his neck and rings on his fingers, (which weren't necessarily gold. In fact, they probably amounted to $1.00), and alligator shoes with sweat socks. You get the picture. As the

81

games progressed, everyone got in a real party mood. Marvin Gaye was blasting on the stereo, *"Let's get it on. O-o-o-o Baby. Let's get it on..."* "C'mon girl. That's my song," Dad said, as he grabbed Geraldine and started dancing. They all got up and started dancing, taking a break from the game.

Mr. Russell had a lot of money that he left in stacks of $20 , $10 and $5 bills on the table, while he was dancing. I looked around to see if anyone was looking my way, including Greg. I peeped in Dad's bedroom, and Greg and Marlin were playing Atari games. So I slowly edged toward the game table, like a cat stealthily stalking its prey. I quickly snatched a $20, a $10 and a $5 bill from each stack, folded them in my hand, and went to the bathroom. Then I put the money in my bra, which I always kept on, even at night when I slept. While I still hated the stench of alcohol, it was commonplace at these parties, and everyone was so drunk, that I knew the money would not be missed. So now I had the money to go home, because it costs $30.00 for a one-way ticket. I just needed to figure out *how* and *when* I'd go.

That following Monday, my dad enrolled Greg and me in school. He drove us every morning to school. That first day of school was horrendous. As if it weren't bad enough that we had to live in Death Valley, the schools there turned out to be battlefields. "Y'all in Gang Central now," Dad proclaimed, with a slight chuckle. "But you ain't seen nothin' yet, until you see the high school up the street. So y'all be careful," he said.

Lawrence Dunbar Middle School had bars on all the windows, and there were metal detectors, which Security used to search each person before entering the school. Everyone had to be buzzed in by Security. I noticed, as we walked through the halls, that a lot of kids wore red or blue bandanas over their noses and mouths like bank robbers, making it so you could only see their eyes. (Yes, these kids had control of this school to the point that they were allowed to wear these kerchiefs over their noses and mouths, and *no one* stopped them.) When they passed each other in the hallways, they greeted each other with strange hand signals.

"Dad, is everybody deaf in this school? Will I have to learn sign language?" I asked, naively, since I had never before seen kids using their hands to signal their gang affiliations. I looked over at Greg, and he was shaking his head, as if to say, *You so dumb, Shelley. You don't know nothin'!* "Remember I told you this was Gang Central? Well, red is the color of the Bloods and blue is the color of the Crips gangs. Their hand signals also tell what gang they're from," Dad explained further. "I sure am glad I wore yellow today," I said, thinking that would mean I would be treated OK by everybody. Dad enrolled me and walked me to my classroom. "I'll be here to pick you up after school, so just wait for me close to the bus stop. OK?" "OK", I answered, feeling strange and apprehensive. "Greg, you come over here to Shelley's school and wait with her for me to pick y'all up after school, since your high school is just up the block." "Alright," Greg said, almost in a daze, as if he didn't believe we were in this place *at all*. After Dad dropped me off at my classroom, he and Greg went to W. E. B. DuBois High School up the street, where he was enrolled.

Attending Lawrence Dunbar Middle School could only be described as appalling and horrific! As the *new* girl, I had to contend with most of the boys wanting to befriend me, or take me out, because they thought I was cute. This meant that the first boy who took me out would be the "chillest" according to the silly games that they played. I always had long, black hair, when I was younger, so boys, both younger and older, were always attracted to me. However, I was also very skinny—no more than ninety-five pounds. On the other hand, the *girls* took it upon themselves to make sure I was harassed, letting me know, in no uncertain terms, not to mess with their boyfriends. I think they were jealous that the boys looked at me and wanted to talk to me. They said, "Look how skinny she is, and her butt is as flat as an ironing board."(Well, they were telling the *truth* about one thing. I never did have much of a back-side.) So, every day, going through the hallways, I looked straight ahead, as I walked, ignoring their taunts.

It was Friday, and when I entered the classroom, I found that it was total chaos in the room. Kids were throw-ing paper around the room at one another, throwing papers at the teacher, who was at the blackboard, and yelling across the room at one another. "Yo', there's the new girl." someone yelled out. As I made my way to my seat, I had to pass Justin and his girlfriend Shirley's desks, since they sat right next to each other. Shirley turned her head to talk with the girl behind her, and, at the same time, Justin winked his eye at me. Just at that time, Shirley turned around and said, "Justin, what you lookin' at? I know you ain't lookin at Miss Skinny Ass," she said, as she rolled her eyes at me and slowly drew her finger across her neck, as if to say, *I will cut your throat if you even think about messin' with my man.* I quickly got in my seat and made sure I didn't look in either one of their directions. I just wanted to be left alone, and bide my time until I could get out of there and go home. The last thing on my mind was fooling with these deadbeats. Shirley and all these other girls truly had noth-ing to worry about. My man, Jerome, ran circles around these "wanna be's," and I was going to get back to him sooner rather than later!

As we did every morning, my brother and I set out to go to school, but *this* time, when my father dropped us off at school, I was determined that this would be the *last* time I would see him, at least that was what I had planned. I had been miserable for those few weeks that I was in Detroit, and I felt that I had jumped from the skillet into the frying pan! So, as quickly as Dad dropped me off, and drove on, I turned back around, never even going inside the school building. Instead, I walked down to the Qwik Stop on the corner to get a snack to take with me to the bus station. It was frigid cold outside that day, and the snow looked like, and felt like, it was ten feet deep. I had on some gray sweat pants that were too thin to act as a barrier to the bone-chilling cold, a thin jacket, and old, worn sneakers. But none of that mattered. I had made up my mind I was leaving this foul place forever! And, as luck would have it, there in the Qwik Stop, I ran into good, ol' Mr. Russell, still wearing all his chains and rings. In fact, I think he was wearing one or two *more* chains around his neck! "Hi, Shelley. What you doin' here. Ain't you supposed to be in school right now?" he asked. "My dad didn't tell you that I'm leaving Detroit and going home today?" "Naw, he didn't say nothin' about it to *me*," Mr. Russell said. "Well, I just had to drop off my last paper at school, and was going to take a cab to the bus station, but I was a little hungry and thought I should get something to eat on the bus before I go. But now that you're here, do you have time to take me to the bus station? I'll give *you* the money I was going to give to the cab driver." "Well, yeah, I got time," Mr., Russell said. "First I need to stop at the apartment and pick up my bag. Is that alright?" "Sure, Shelley. It's on the way, so no problem." Then I chuckled inside, because I was thinking, *Wow! He is so naïve!*

I ran into the apartment, quickly grabbed my bag, that had never really been fully unpacked, and rode to the bus terminal with Mr. Russell. That seemed like the longest ride ever. My hands were sweating and I was anxious, just hoping and praying that nothing would stop me from getting on that bus. I paid him, and was getting out of the car when Mr. Russell said, "That's a long way for a young girl like you to be goin' by yourself," he said with that cigarette hanging from the corner of his lips, like it always did. "I'll be alright, Mr. Russell, 'cause my mom's going to meet me, and the bus driver always looks out for kids that are traveling." "OK, Lil' Lady. I'll see you next time you come," Mr. Russell said as I walked into the bus terminal. I waved to him, thinking, *You ain't gonna' ever see me again, Mr. Russell, 'cause I ain't never comin' back here, ever!"* Then I quickly purchased my ticket back to Randall to go home.

When I got on the bus, and was making myself comfortable, a young lady sat down right next to me. "Hi, Sweetie, my name is Shelley Ann. What's your name?" I smiled and said, "That's my name, too, Shelley Ann," I answered proudly. "St-o-o-o-p! Really?" she asked, smiling. "Yeah, we got the same name," I answered full of wonder and excitement. She was a beautiful, black lady, with a head full of hair, and a prominent gold tooth just to the side of her front teeth. After introducing ourselves, we both remarked about the coincidence of having the same names. She told me she was headed to Pittsburgh. Then she asked how old I was, and I told her I was thirteen. She questioned, "Why are you riding this bus alone? You're going to be on the bus for at least sixteen hours. Did you know that?" "Yeah. Just a few weeks ago, I made this same trip, so I know it's a long one." I also told her that my mother was going to meet me in Randall, just as I told Mr. Russell, and she just nodded her head. I felt very safe with her for the long trip home, and was glad that she had shown concern for me. It was as if God had sent an angel to watch over me for those sixteen hours. The fear and lack of trust of adults, which I had harbored for such a long time, just seemed to disappear regarding this kind lady. I'll never forget how she made my ride back home so much more pleasant.

Chapter 6

When I reached Randall, I took a cab from the bus station and went to the last place I knew my mother was living. I saw some neighbors and was told by them that she had moved and, also with whom she was living now. The cab driver was very patient, as he drove me around, trying to locate her. And I was so happy when we finally found her! I wanted to see her so badly. She was living with a friend of hers, along with my sister (who was back from Illinois) and my little brother, Derrick, in a two-bedroom apartment. (Greg stayed in Detroit, living with Dad, Geraldine and Marlin.) With my luggage in hand, I ran up the stairs to see her.

I knocked on the door, lightly, and thought *Finally, I'll get to see Momma and know, for sure, that Dad just made up that story about that adoption thing. She wouldn't leave us with a man we didn't know, let alone in a house as crazy as his was. I know she wouldn't.* When the door opened, and I saw my mother standing there, I was shocked. She did not look the same. In fact, she had the look of death on her face, both the look of death from her drug addiction, and the look of death like she wanted to *kill* me. If looks could kill! Her eyes had that glaze that addicts have, and she was as thin as a rail. She looked awful. All that would come out of my mouth was, "Hi, Momma." She asked me how I had gotten there, and I told her. Then she invited me in and just stared at me, as I sat down, very slowly, not knowing what else to say. "You cain't stay here," she said sternly, totally devoid of the joy and love I thought would be there when she saw me again. She might as well have stuck a dagger in my heart, or taken a gun and shot me. The pain couldn't have been worse. *My mother don't want me in her home, in her heart, or in her life anymore. Where am I gonna' go? What am I gonna' do? Dad wasn't lyin' after all. She really don't want me! What did I do to make her hate me like this?* I kept puzzling over this, trying to figure out what had just happened to me, and what I should do next. "Where's Derrick, and how *is* he?" I asked. "Derrick's fine. Don't you worry about Derrick. Ya' betta' be worryin' about yo'self, 'cause I know yo' fast tail is gonna' still fool around with that bastard Jerome, like ya' ain't got no sense. Ya' think ya' grown, but ya' ain't, Shelley. But since ya' wanna' act like ya' grown, then just git on out there and be grown. Just look afta' *yo'self*! Look, ya' gotta' go, 'cause my girlfriend will be home soon, and this is her place. She ain't gonna' take too kindly to seein' you here, thinkin' I'm tryin' to move someone else in here."

So she went to the door and opened it, signaling for me to leave. I got up slowly, picked up my bag and walked out the open door. "Bye, Momma. I love you," I said through the waterfall of tears that were just about to brim over from my eyes. She just looked at me with sad, drug-filled eyes and said nothing, as she closed the door, practically in my face.

I just stood there for a moment. Then I'm so sure I heard her say, through the door, "Bye Shelley," as she was weeping.

"I'm so sorry, Baby. But you gotta' look in the right place for the love you're seekin'. Now c'mon over here and hug me," Jackie said. Then she was gone. Then I remembered my friend from school, Michelle, lived with her mother and sister, Brenda, not too far from where my mother was staying. So I left and went over to her apartment. It just so happened that she lived in the same apartment complex as my mother, so I didn't have far to walk. She asked her mother, Mrs. Davis, if I could sleep over. Her mother looked me over very suspiciously, but then said I could stay. Then Mrs. Davis said to Michelle, "Come in here. I need to talk to you a minute." They went to another room, but. I could still hear Mrs. Davis saying, "She can't stay here long. Look at her hair, and why is she dressed like that?" "But Momma, she doesn't have any place else to go tonight. Can't she just stay tonight?" Michelle pleaded. "Alright. But she's got to go tomorrow. I mean that, you hear me?" "Yes ma'am. Thank you, Momma."

Mrs. Davis was a hair stylist, and she taught her two daughters to be stylists, as well. She was actually giving a perm to a client when I arrived at her apartment. She was a full-bodied woman, with large hips, and the longest fingernails I'd ever seen. Jeri Curls were the rage then, as I said earlier, and she had one herself. She was quite the diva, and looked at me as if I were the scum of the earth. In fact, she really didn't want her daughters to associate with me, because she didn't think I was at their level. So the very next day, I called the man I just *knew* would not deny me. I was in love with my Jerome, and he loved me. I told him about all that took place with my mother, what happened in Detroit, and explained why I spent the night with Michelle.

"Brown Suga', you shoulda' called me right away. Ya' know ya' always got a place with me." He wasted no time in coming to pick me up. "C'mere Brown Suga', he said, grabbing me and hugging and kissing me. At last, somebody was glad to see me! He picked up my luggage, as we walked down the stairs to the car, and I thought he was the perfect gentleman. "Whose car is that?" I asked as we neared it. "It's my mom's car. She just bought it a couple of weeks ago," he explained. When we reached the car, I no-

89

ticed a couple of his friends were in the back seat. They all
reeked of alcohol, which really came as no surprise to me,
because Jerome and his friends always drank a lot. But
none of that mattered to me, at that moment. Shortly, we
arrived at Jerome's mother's house, where he stayed.

When Mrs. Washington saw me, it was very clear by
the look on her face that she was not happy to see me.
"Jerome, where you been? I've been waitin' for over an
hour for you to bring me that sugar." "I had to pick up
Shelley, Mom. But here's the sugar. I didn't forget it, and
your change is in the bag." "Hi Mrs. Washington", I said
meekly. "Hi, Shelley. How you doin', Baby?" "I'm alright," I said. Mrs. Washington yanked the bag from
Jerome's hands, and started toward the house. The aroma
of fried chicken was wafting all through the house. I hadn't
tasted good, home-cooked, juicy fried chicken, greens,
sweet potatoes and corn bread in so long that my mouth
began to water as we entered the house. Jerome said, "Have
a seat, Baby. I need to talk with Momma about somethin'.
Do you want somethin' to eat or drink? Dinner should be
ready pretty soon." "That's alright. I can wait for dinner," I
said. Jerome went in the kitchen and talked to Mrs. Washington for a few minutes. Then he came back, turned on the
television, and just held me. His friends had made themselves at home on the porch, knowing that Mrs. Washington would not fail to invite them to dinner too, like she always did. "Y'all c'mon and eat, " Mrs. Washington called
out. We all sat down at the table, and after Mrs. Washington said grace, we started passing the food around. It
looked so good! I bit into that fried chicken leg like I'd
never eaten in life. I was starved, and my growling stomach
was a testimony to how hungry I was. Those collard greens
were the best I'd ever tasted in my entire life. I was eating
so fast, I was barely chewing the food. I think I swallowed
a good deal of it whole.

All of a sudden, my stomach started churning, and I felt
like the food was going to all come up. I ran to the bath-

room, feeling totally nauseous, and lost all the food I had just eaten. It seemed like I'd never stop! Finally, I washed out my mouth and wiped my face. Then I came back out of the bathroom. "Shelley, you sick, Honey? You runnin' a fever?" Mrs. Washington asked, with a strange and knowing look on her face. "No ma'am. I don't have a fever," I answered. "You're not pregnant, are ya', Shelley?" she probed more. "No ma'am. Me and Jerome ain't done nothin.'" "Girl, don't you fix your mouth to tell that lie! I wasn't born yesterday! Jerome, first thing tomorrow mornin', you take Shelley to that clinic, and you betta' pray she ain't pregnant." "Aw, Momma, ain't nobody pregnant," Jerome said. "Well you just take her to that clinic out there on Grant Street. Look in my purse and get out $5.00 to pay for her pregnancy test there. Then we'll know for sure," she said, slowly shaking her head. Then she went back in the kitchen, and started cleaning up the dishes from dinner.

"Let's go out to the car so I can rap to you for a minute, Brown Suga,'" Jerome said. We got in the car and he said, "When's the last time you had your period?" he said, almost like he was mad. His tone of voice surprised me and made me shudder a little bit. "I don't know. Maybe 3 or 4 months ago," I answered. "Three or four months ago? Look, I ain't ready to be nobody's daddy. I'm just 17 years old! Why in the hell didn't you tell me when you first missed your period so we could do somethin' about it?" "What do you mean do somethin' about it? Like what?" I asked, naively. "Maybe you *are* too young for me, like Momma's been sayin', 'cause if you don't know the answer to *that* question, you dumb as a box of rocks," he said sarcastically. "Well, if I *am* pregnant, then that must make *two* of us that are dumb, 'cause I didn't get pregnant by myself," I answered defiantly. Then he kinda looked at me and said, "I'm sorry, Baby. I'm just trippin'. This was so sudden. I mean, I wasn't thinkin' that I'd have a baby when I just graduated from high school. I had my whole future ahead of me, and havin' a baby wasn't in that picture? Ya' feel me?" "I guess," I answered, still not sure what to make of his angry outburst just a moment ago. "Look. My mom's cool people, but she's still ol' school. She's gonna' let you stay here in the spare room, and I'll sleep downstairs, for a few days 'til we can figure somethin' out. Now let's forget about all this for now, and have some fun. I'm really glad to see you. Why don't you go upstairs and freshen up, 'cause my boy, Andre's, havin' a party tonight. OK?" So I went upstairs and tried to get as pretty as I could. I really didn't want to think about whether or not I was pregnant, although I did feel something was going on, and my body was changing. I just didn't know why.

That night, Andre had the whole house to himself, because his parents were out of town. There were wall-to-wall people upstairs and downstairs in every room of the house. There was a $2.00 cover charge at the door, but because Jerome was a popular DJ in town, and Andre was his best friend, we got in for free. The house was very dark, other than a few red lights shining throughout. Curtis Blow was blasting on the stereo, *"These are the breaks..."* Everybody was doing the Flintstones dance, because it was all the rage, at that time. I was so glad to be back home, partying with my man! I hadn't been that happy in a long time. Tequila was flowing like water, and Jerome was gulping down shots as fast as they could refill his glass. Then, he took his lighter and set fire to the Tequila. "Drink this down through this straw, Brown Suga'. It'll relax ya', and make you feel good," Jerome instructed me. I had never drunk alcohol before, so this was my first time even tasting it. "But, Jerome. There's fire in there. I'll burn myself," I protested. He started laughing and said, "No you won't, Baby. Would I tell you to do somethin' that would hurt you?" he said, slurring his words. So I did what he asked me to do. I did what he said, and it felt like a hole had burnt through my chest! I was on fire, from my mouth, down my throat, through my chest, to my stomach! I'll never forget how much that burnt! I started coughing and I couldn't stop. I tried to make my way to the kitchen through the crowd. When I finally got there, I ran to the sink, leaned over and drank as much water from the faucet as I could. I was on fire! "Are you OK, Shelley?" Andre said, concerned. "I feel really sick, and my stomach is killin' me." "Hold on. Let me go get Jerome," Andre said, and he rushed to find Jerome. Within a short time, Andre and Jerome showed up in the kitchen. "Aw, man. Chill! She'll be alright," Jerome said, without the slightest concern for me.

Then a sharp pain hit me so hard that I doubled over. "Andre, where's the bathroom?" "Here, I'll take you Shelley." Andre maneuvered me through the crowd as fast as he could. I closed the door to the bathroom quickly because I felt like I was peeing on myself. When I took down my panties, they were drenched with blood, and the pains kept getting worse. I was scared to death! "Andre, are you still there?" I yelled through the door. "Yeah, Shelley. You alright?" "I'm really bleedin,' Andre, and I'm scared. I need to go to the hospital, but Jerome's too drunk to drive me. Can you take me?" "Yeah, I'll take you, Shelley. You know I will. C'mon. Let's go." As Andre led me out the door, I looked over and saw Jerome knocked out on a chair. That night, I really began to see Jerome in a different light. He wasn't really there for me. Thank God, his best friend, Andre, was more caring.

I had a miscarriage and lost the baby that night. Andre contacted Jerome's mother to come and sign for me, and she did. When I awakened that next morning, she was sitting at my bedside. I just looked at her and began crying, from sheer exhaustion, and, an incredible sense of sorrow and loss at losing my baby. He was a boy, and they had let me hold his little, lifeless body for just a little while. That was enough time for me to bond with my child, and grieve at the thought that I would never be able to love him and watch him grow. So, Mrs. Washington just held me and let me cry, and told me everything would be alright. As Mrs. Washington was holding me, I looked toward the end of the bed, and my lady Jackie was standing there, weeping, as I was. She didn't say a word, I guess because Mrs. Washington was already comforting me. But just seeing her there was enough to let me know, she still loved me. And that was what I needed more than anything.

Jerome came to the hospital with flowers, and said he was sorry for what had happened. But something in me had changed. Seeing him drunk and passed out at that party, with no concern for me or our baby's welfare, had turned me off to the extent that I felt very distant from him, and didn't want to be bothered with him. I had begun to see him for what he was, an immature, selfish alcoholic, who still lived with his mother and who cared about himself much more than he cared about me or anyone else. After the miscarriage, I went back to Mrs. Washington's house to recuperate, because I had no place else to go, at the time. Mrs. Washington was kind to me, but Jerome became more and more argumentative and abusive. He started fighting with me and beating me on a regular basis, but I felt I had no place else to turn. But let's be clear here. It wasn't as if I'd just *let* Jerome use me as a punching bag. No, not by a long shot, because before his strength overtook me, I'd fight back with all my might. And there were a few times, because he was so drunk he couldn't defend himself, I got the better of *him*!

One time, we were at a party, and, as usual, Jerome drank too much and became loud and rowdy. "Jerome, let's go home. I'm, gettin' tired," I told him, really more fed up with his drunkenness than tired "Sit down and shut the hell up! I ain't ready to go. I shoulda' left your dumb butt at home," Jerome growled. "Jerome, c'mon," I urged, "before you get too loaded to drive us home." The next thing I knew I was on the floor from the blow he had just given me across my face "Take your slow behind on outta' here and walk home, if you so ready to go. And leave me the hell alone," Jerome yelled at me, getting ready to hit me again. When I saw him raise his fist that time, I used all I had seen on TV and in the movies and quickly kicked my leg out, like a Black Belt in Karate, to land strategically in his balls!! "That's right, Shelley, my Girl! Kick him again for me," Jackie said, laughing and making moves like a boxer. I knew I had him then, because he couldn't even get up off the floor. In fact, he was coughing and wheezing and gasping for breath. The music had stopped, and everyone was gathered around us. Everyone at the party was cheering for *me*, and the guys were busting out laughing. Even his friend, Andre, had a slight smile on his face. You see, everyone knew us, and knew how he had treated me so badly in the past. No one was defending him. In fact, their concern was for *me*. One of the girls, Eileen, asked if I was alright, and told me she'd give me a ride home. That was a turning point for me, and I fought him, at every turn, from that moment on! Yes, I had developed some confidence and a little moxie, because I didn't idolize Jerome anymore. But, the daily harangues and fights, and beatings finally took their toll on me. I just couldn't take it anymore.

So, one day, when I was in the bathroom, after he had beaten me pretty badly, I looked in the mirror and started saying to myself, *Shelley MacDonald, you poor, dumb, pitiful fool. Here you are, 13 years old, already been "knocked up" and lost a baby. Your baby's daddy is a sorry excuse for a man, who stays drunk, and beats the hell out of you whenever he feels like it. You don't even know where your momma is. Ya' got nowhere else to go. Ya' just got a 6th grade education, but you've dropped out of school already, and you're too young to get a decent payin' job. Ya' livin' in this Hell Hole, but you don't have no money to get out and live someplace else. Ya' may not even be able to have more kids 'cause the doctors in the hospital said your blood type is Rh negative, and if you did have another child, it might be born with some birth defects. I just don't see what you waitin' around for, Girlfriend. Go on and stop all this sufferin'. You don't have to keep livin' like this, where ya' can't even see a way out. End it now and get relieved from*

*all this hurt and heartache. Nobody cares, anyway. Ya'
gotta' be tired of all this, right?*

Shaky, sweaty, hurting and exhausted from fighting
with Jerome, I saw a person I didn't know or recognize, in
the mirror. Her hair was all over her head. Her lip was
bleeding and busted. Her arms and neck were bruised. Her
eyes had dark circles under them, and her blouse was
ripped and torn. She reminded me of my momma after she
and Phil, the monster, had tussled. *Is that where I'm headed
– tryin' to escape from life by druggin' myself up, like
Momma? Is that all that's left for me?* As I pondered these
questions, I slowly and calmly opened the medicine cabinet
door. I took out a small box of razor blades, and took one
blade from the box. I looked back at myself one last time in
the mirror. Then, I took that razor blade and slashed my left
wrist as hard as I could! I yelled out because the pain was
so severe it caught me off guard. Blood began gushing out
of my wrist in great torrents. I just watched it flow, almost
as if I was watching someone else.

"Shelley, are you alright?" Mrs. Washington shouted,
as she banged on the bathroom door. She sounded alarmed
and panicked. "Shelley, open the door. I heard you yell out.
Let me in.," she ordered. "Go away, Mrs. Washington. I'll
be alright," I said, feeling a little light-headed. "Shelley
MacDonald, this is my house, and I have a key to every
room in this house, so I will get in, one way or the other.
Now you open this door this minute!" she demanded. I
slowly walked to the door, with blood dripping all over the
bathroom floor, and unlocked the door. Mrs. Washington
swung the door open so fast, she almost knocked me down.
"Oh my God, Shelley. What have you done?" She started
grabbing towels, wet them and wrapped them around my
wrist, as tight as she could, as she pressed down hard on the
slash in my wrist. "Now you c'mon and let's get you to
Emergency," she said grabbing her purse and keys and putting me in the car. I didn't protest because I just didn't have
any energy left to do so. In fact, I was beginning to feel like

I would faint. Mrs. Washington kept talking to me in the car all the way to the hospital, but I don't remember a word she said. By the time we reached Emergency, I had passed out.

I woke about 2:00 a.m., still in a daze. When I got my bearings, and realized I was in a hospital room, I saw Mrs. Washington sitting in the chair over in the corner. She was sound asleep. "My sweet, sweet, Shelley. I'm so glad you're still here. I'd been waitin' for ya' to call on me, but ya' didn't. Why didn't you, Baby?" Jackie said, with more hurt than disappointment in her voice. She was standing right beside me, holding my hand and stroking my forehead. Mrs. Washington was in such a deep sleep that she didn't hear her, apparently. "I was so 'shamed, Jackie, 'cause everything you told me and tried to warn me about was how things turned out with Jerome. I was 'shamed 'cause I didn't listen to ya', and I thought ya' wouldn't want to be bothered with me again," I said, beginning to cry softly. "Aw, Shelley, Baby, even though I mighta' been displeased and disappointed in ya', that didn't mean that I didn't love ya'. And it certainly didn't mean that I would judge ya' or ever leave ya'. I'm gonna' always be here for you, Shelley, whether you listen to me or not. And if there's any distance between us, it's because you may need to go through some of life's learnin's on your own to really understand them. Shelley, I've been right here all along, watchin' ya' fall deeper and deeper into your own darkness, but I couldn't pull ya' up unless you wanted me to. Ya' see? But now, Shelley, ya' eyes are open, and ya' breathin' this mornin, so what does that tell ya'?" "That I'm not dead, yet, and that there's hope for a better tomorrow," I said, only half believing it. "A-a-a-a-men! But ya' gotta' say it with a lot more belief and faith than ya' just did in order for it to be *your* truth, Shelley, Girl." "But, Jackie, I got no place to go, no money, I'm just thirteen. I just don't see what's gonna' happen to change all this," "How your tomorrow is gonna' be better is a question I can't even answer for ya', Shelley. But I know it will be better, just like you gotta' know it will, and walk in that truth, as if it's already here. Then, you'll see things start to change for ya'. But you also hafta' to stop bein' your own worst enemy, Baby. What I mean is, you gotta' change your mind about who ya' *are* and what ya' *want* out of this life, and stop settlin' for these no-account, low-life people that ya' associate with. I know ya' young, Shelley, but ya' old enough now, 'specially with all you been through, to start makin' better choices about the people you want in your life. Nothin' will get better for ya' if *you* don't change, Suga'. Now that Mrs. Washington is a good woman, Shelley, who really does want the best for you. But her son don't have her character. So you'll need to leave her house, as soon as you can, after you leave this hospital. I know ya' think ya' don't have no place to go, right now, but, I guarantee you, somethin' will turn up, and a way will be made for ya' to move from that house and get away from Jerome, so you can start fresh. Trust me. And as far as ya' checkin' out of this life 'cause ya' feel ya' got no hope, that ain't gonna' happen until it's time for ya' to go, Sweetie. And it wasn't your time last night, 'cause here it is, the next day and..." "I'm not dead yet, and I'm still breathin'," we both yelled so loud in unison that we had to laugh. "That's my Shelley talkin,'" Jackie said, with that big, brilliant smile that lights up a whole room. "And don't you forget it! Now c'mon over here and let me hug you close for a minute before I leave." So Jackie held me and rocked me, humming some sweet song, that sounded really familiar, but I couldn't put my finger on where I'd heard it before. And before long, I was asleep, again, feeling more peace than I had felt in a long time.

Chapter 7

"Shelley, Honey, I'm so sorry about all that ya' been goin' through. And it's takin' all the strength I got to keep from gettin' my gun and shootin' Jerome myself 'cause of the way he's treated you. But, Baby, ain't no man, includin' my son, worth killin' yourself over. Ya' hear? So don't ya' ever let any man bring you down that far again. Now, ya' kinda' weak, right now, and ya' need to get your strength back, so I'm lettin' ya' stay with me a little longer. But, once you get yo' strength back, we need to look for someplace else for ya' to live, and ya' tell my son to kiss yo' ass! I mean that," Mrs. Washington said with fervor and conviction. "Now at the hospital, they started askin' a lot of questions about ya', and I pretended to be yo' foster parent, otherwise, they were gonna' take ya' and put ya' in that system, where ya' might end up bein' even worse off than ya' already are. So, I convinced 'em that we'd keep these appointments they set up with this doctor, and this shrink. And frankly, Shelley, after all you been through, it might not be a bad idea for you to go to these appointments. OK? While you're getting' better, though, we'll start lookin' to find you someplace to go where you'll be safe."

"Thanks, Mrs. Washington. I 'preciate all you doin' for me," I told her with all the sincere gratitude I could muster. "Well, it's OK, Shelley. Ya' really been dealt some tough cards in yo' young life, Baby, but ya' gonna' need to continue to stay strong. Ya' hear? And you'll make it. I just know ya' will," she told me, while patting my hand.

When we got to her house, Mrs. Washington helped me up the stairs, and put me in the bed in the spare room. Luckily, Jerome was nowhere to be found, because I really didn't want to be bothered with him. Within a few minutes, Mrs. Washington came upstairs with a serving tray holding a bowl of her home-made, chicken noodle soup, crackers, and a glass of milk. "There ain't been a ailment yet that chicken noodle soup and a glass o' milk didn't help heal, 'cause they give ya' back yo' strength and energy. So you go on and eat alla' this and drink all this milk, Shelley, and I'll be back later to pick up the tray. You just rest here today, and tomorrow we'll start workin' on where ya' go from here. Now, mind ya', I'm not kickin' ya' out in the street tomorrow, 'cause you still need a few more days to get better, but we just gonna' start thinkin' about and plannin' for when ya' *do* leave." "Thanks, Mrs. Washington. This sure looks good," I told her, anxious to sample, once again, food prepared by the hands of the greatest cook I'd ever known.

"That hospital food sure was nasty," I said, turning up my nose. "I know, Baby. So you just eat this all up. There's more downstairs if ya' want some more," she said, chuckling as she left the room. I had never before seen anyone who got as much joy as Mrs. Washington did from cooking good food and having people really enjoy it. I wondered if I'd ever be a cook like her. After, I scarfed down the soup and milk, I went to sleep and didn't awaken until the next morning.

Over the next few days, I began to feel healthier and stronger. Jerome was in and out, and he tried to get back into my good graces by being very attentive to my needs and very solicitous. He brought me flowers, practically every day, and wouldn't let me lift a finger to do anything. And though I knew this Jerome could change to the worthless, selfish Jerome, on a dime, I *did* enjoy the attention, and realized I hadn't pushed him completely out of my system. Nevertheless, I was determined to find somewhere else to go, as soon as possible. It had been some time since I had seen Momma, and I suddenly had a great yearning to see her. Mrs. Washington and I made a few calls and found that she was living in the basement of one of her friends' homes in Templeton, Maryland. Her friend's name was Margaret Winston, and we had no trouble finding her phone number. So I called her, and after we talked, she told me I was welcome to come and stay in the basement with my mother. Mrs. Washington was somewhat apprehensive about my going to live with my mother, because she knew how deeply addicted Momma had become to crack cocaine. But I convinced her that I'd be alright, and she reluctantly drove me to Ms. Winston's house and dropped me off.

As it turned out, Ms. Winston's house was in a section of Templeton that was very near one of the worst, drug-infested areas in Maryland. When she answered the door, however, she welcomed me in, warmly, and showed me down to the basement where I'd be staying. Momma wasn't there, at the time, so I made myself at home, and tried to settle in. I didn't want to stay there long, because of the area of the city the house was located in, but this was a place to lay my head, for now.

Momma didn't come home all that day, so, the next morning, I asked Ms. Winston if she knew where Momma was. She dropped her head, slightly, then looked me in the eye and said, "Yeah, Shelley. I know where she is. She's over at The Gardens, so ya' might not see her for a long time, or she could pop in here any time now. I never know," Ms. Winston said, matter-of-factly. "But ya' promise me, Shelley, that ya' won't go over there tryin' to find her, 'cause it's too dangerous over there. You know why, don't ya'?" she asked. "Yeah. That's where the place is filled with crack addicts," I answered sadly. "That's right, Shelley. And yo' momma is deep in that life, but don't you go near it. Ya' hear me? Now, I ain't no saint, myself, and I take me a hit or two, now and then, sometimes wit' yo' momma. I'm just bein' truthful. But, I'm still workin' and makin' my way. Yo' momma, on the other hand, has lost her way, right now, Shelley, and she'll have to find her way back. That's why she's just in and out o' here in the basement, so it's no problem lettin' you stay down there for a little bit. Now, ya' welcome ta' use the phone, but just don't put any long distance calls on my bill. And any food you see in the house ya' want, feel free to have it, cook it, whatever, as long as ya' make sure ya' leave some for me and yo' momma, in case she should come home. I'm lettin' ya' stay here, Shelley, 'cause ya' Gladys' daughta', and I'd do anythin' for Gladys 'cause she stuck wit' me and helped me out one time when I really needed a friend. That's why I let her stay here, an' now I'm lettin' you stay here, for a while. OK? Let me know if ya' need anythin' else." "Ms. Winston, do ya' mind if I take a shower?" I asked, still sadly mulling over what she had told me about Momma. "You go right ahead, Shelley. The clean towels and linen are in that linen closet right outside the bathroom. Now, I'm gonna' go out for a bit, Shelley, so I'll see ya' later." "Bye, Ms. Winston. Thanks, again."

Luckily, Ms. Winston had really hot water that didn't run cold quickly. So I took a lengthy shower, relishing the feel of the hot, steamy water propelling, at full force, against my skin. It felt so good! And I imagined that I was on some exotic island, standing naked, directly under the most dazzling, blue waterfall, cleansing my body with huge palm leaves, and the largest, most beautiful orchids and gardenias the world had ever seen, whose fragrance punctuated the air and clung to my body. In reality, I was using Ms. Winston's shower gel and shampoo, alternating between the orchid and gardenia fragrances. I washed my thick hair and conditioned it with reckless abandon, not caring how it would look once it dried. It felt so good and smelled so good that I wasn't going to sweat the small stuff.

After drying myself, and applying lotion all over my body, I looked through the drawers and cabinets in the bathroom and found a hair jell which I generously applied to my damp hair. Then I brushed and combed it back, and tied it down with a scarf, as tight as I could. I looked at myself in the full length mirror, fully examining my body from head to toe, and thought, *Shelley MacDonald. You fine, Girl! And you gonna' be alright!* Now, I don't think that I'd ever really thought about myself in that way, though others had said these things to me all my life. So this was, indeed, the beginning of a different Shelley!

As I sat around in my robe, I started to get bored. Then, I happened to think that I hadn't talked with my girlfriend, Michelle or her sister, Brenda, in a long time. I knew Michelle's number by heart, so I called her. She was so excited to hear from me, and said she and Brenda were going out that night, and asked if I wanted to go with them. Now, both Michelle and her sister were several years older than me, and when she told me they were going to a club, I reminded her that I didn't have an I.D. She said, "No problem," and told me she'd pick me up in an hour. I ran and got dressed in what I thought was my best and sexiest outfit. And when I took that scarf off my head, to my great surprise, my hair was just a cascade of beautiful, natural waves that I left hanging below my shoulders, down my back. I inspected myself one last time in the mirror, and smiled with satisfaction and confidence.

Being Jerome's girl, I had gotten into some smaller neighborhood clubs in Randall, but *this* club was *huge*, and it was in Baltimore. The club was called *Escape*, and there was a long line of people all around the corner, waiting to get in. "Michelle, how long are we gonna' have to wait in line in these heels before we git in?" I asked, concerned about how my feet were going to feel if we had a long wait. Michelle and Brenda looked at each other and laughed. When they stopped, Michelle said, "Look, Shell, you with us. We don't wait in line. We *got* it like that. Just relax and follow us. OK, Girl?" "Aw, so y'all got the hook up, eh? My bad! I'm rollin' with y'all then," I said, as we all chuckled, slightly smirking. And just as Michelle had said, we walked straight up to the bouncer, who was on the door, and he said, "Good evening, Ladies. You certainly look beautiful tonight. I think you've outdone yourself, Ms. Michelle. Mr. Tipton will be pleased. And who do we have *here*?" he said, pointing to me. "This is my girl, Shelley. We grew up together, but hadn't seen each other for a while, so, of course, we wanted to bring her to our favorite spot in the entire world," Michelle said, convincingly. "Well, you know if she's *your* girl, she's always welcome here. Welcome to *Escape*, Miss Shelley. Enjoy your evening," he said, as he opened the door and ushered us in.

"That was Reuben. Ain't he fine? But he ain't worth a quarter, Girl. And he ain't that good in bed either. I know. I had him," Brenda declared. "Girl, shut up! There ain't too many men in here you haven't had. You oughtta' be ashamed of yourself for bein' such a ho'. If you weren't my sister, and I didn't love ya', I wouldn't even hang with you," Michelle said, laughing all through her diatribe. "You just jealous 'cause they didn't want *you*, Michelle. Now go on and admit it. Tell the truth," Brenda said, still laughing. "You know, you *right*, Big Sister, I really just wish I was you. You right," Michele said, almost tripping over the carpet in the entrance because she was laughing so hard. "I see y'all still as crazy as ya' always was," I chimed in, laughing as hard as they were. "Shell, you know we're gonna' always keep it real, 'cause Brenda will always be Brenda, and I will always be Michelle, as different as night and day, but sisters to the end." "That's right, Shell. I might talk about my sister, but I dare anyone else to say one bad thing about her, 'cause it's *on*, if they do. And I ain't playin' about that," Brenda said with gusto. "Me, too, Big Sis. You know I got your back too," Michelle said, leaning over and hugging Brenda. "And now that you're back in the Land of the Livin', Shell, you're in the clan, Little Sis, and we both got your back too," Michelle said. Then, hugging me and Brenda at once, she yelled, "Sistah hug-g-g!"

After going through the long entrance hallway at *Escape*, we finally reached the main area of the club. It was so huge that the small clubs Jerome had taken me to could fit into one small corner of this club. The main dance floor was packed with people dancing, and the music was blasting so loud, you couldn't hear anyone if they said something to you. Michelle took me by the hand and led the way, and Brenda followed me in back. There was a gigantic bar at one end of the first floor, with a huge aquarium as a backdrop. In one section of the aquarium were colorful tropical fish. In another section, there were two women dressed in mermaid costumes, swimming, and coming up for air, periodically. People were stacked, sitting and standing all around the bar, and the tall tables and bar stools adjacent to the bar. Around the perimeter of the first floor were tables and chairs, which were full, as well.

As we walked through, Michelle and Brenda yelled out greetings everywhere we walked. It seemed as if they knew *everybody*. Then we got in a small elevator, and went up to the third floor, marked, "VIP ONLY." When we got out, we went through a beautiful teakwood door, and walked into what looked like the palatial lounge of some wealthy sheik. Beautiful velvet couches, huge ornate sitting pillows, soft shaded lighting, champagne in ice coolers – it was breath-taking! "Well, here's my Lady," an extremely well-dressed, distinguished-looking gentleman said, as he walked over to Michelle and kissed her. "Hi, Brenda. And who do we have here?" he asked, looking in my direction. "Baby, this is Shell. Remember I told you about her? Shelley, this is my baby, Christian. He owns this club. Christian, this is my girl, Shelley, Shell for short," Michelle said, making introductions. "Aw, yes. Welcome, Shell. Come on and have a seat and meet some of the rest of the crew," Christian said, making me feel very welcomed. Then we all sat down, and I was introduced to the other three guys and one woman that were already there. "Let's have champagne, everyone, and celebrate bringing a new member to our crew. A toast to Shelley, Shell, for short. Welcome to *Escape*," Christian said, holding his champagne glass high and motioning to me. I had never felt so special in all my life. *Was I dreaming, or was this for real?* I thanked everyone and sipped the champagne, as we all started chatting. From this third floor vantage point, we could look out over the entire club, and the view was intoxicating.

One of the guys, Aaron, started a conversation with me, and after we had talked for about 15 minutes or so, Michelle asked me to go with her to powder our noses. Now, I don't know whether or not all *men* know this, but we *women* know that when women say, "Let's go powder our noses," what we *really* want is to go somewhere where we can *talk*.

When we got in the Ladies' Restroom, Michelle looked around to make sure no one was in any of the stalls. "Ok, Shell, Girl. Let me tell you what the deal is. The men that you're meetin' now, who are friends of Christian's, my Boo, are all powerful men with money. Now ya' see that white BMW I picked you up in? That's mine, free and clear. That condo I just purchased? It's mine and in my name. My beauty shop I just opened? It's all mine. Christian bought all that for me. And you can have the same things. You're attractive, developed and mature for your age, otherwise you couldn't hang with me. And you're like a little sista' to me, so I'm gonna' teach you all I know. It makes no sense for you to waste your time with a loser like that broke behind, Jerome. Ya' got too much goin' for ya' for that! Listen, all guys got one thing in common. They wanta' sample that sweet stuff," Michelle said bluntly. "What sweet stuff?" I asked naively.

"C'mon, Girl. Wake up. You know what I mean. That sweet stuff between yo' legs. You'd be surprised how much money people will pay for that." "Really?" I said, truly astonished, because I had never placed a value on my womanhood, since others had taken it so freely from me. "Yeah, Shell. Ya' should never *give* this away to *anybody* anymore," she said, placing her hand on top of her womanhood. "Just do what I tell ya' and you'll see what I mean. OK?" "I guess so, Michelle, 'cause you sure are livin' good." Then, we started freshening up our make-up. But when I looked deeper in the mirror, I saw Jackie standing in back of me. She just stood there, shaking her head, with her hands on her hips. I heard her say, "Uh-uh-uh," in a disgusted tone. Then I closed my eyes for a second, and when I opened them, Jackie was gone. Frankly, I didn't want to hear her chastise me, right then, so I put her out of my mind. "Alright, Shell. Let's unbutton that top button and pull that top down, a little," Michelle said as she proceeded to do just that. "One thing you need to learn is that you gotta' work with what you got. And you got nice twins, here, so work 'em, Girl," she said, referring to my generous breasts. Then we started laughing, as we left the restroom.

When we got back to the VIP Lounge, Keith Sweat was blasting over the speakers, *"I want her, I want that girl..."* "That's my jam right there," I said as we arrived back at the tables. "Well, let's see what you got, Shell," Aaron said, directing me to the dance floor. And we danced the night away all night long, from the fastest Flintstones dance to the most intimate, slow dance to one of Luther's greats, *"If this world were mine, I would place at your feet, all that I own, You've been so good to me, If this world were mine..."* Aaron whispered in my ear, "Let's get out of here," he said in that low, sexy baritone voice that gave me chills. But I remembered that Michelle also told me to take it slow and not to make it easy for anyone ever again to sample my sweet stuff. Keeping that in mind, I said, "Not tonight, Aaron. But thanks, anyway." "Alright, Shell, but I *am* gonna' see you again soon, right?" Aaron asked. "I'd like that, Aaron," I said, trying to control my raging hormones. Then I wrote out my phone number and put it in his pocket, as I kissed him on his ear. He looked at me with a knowing smile, signifying that he would definitely be contacting me real soon. And that he did! This man looked so good and smelled so good, I wondered how long I would be able to resist giving him a sample.

On the way home, that morning, after the club had closed, Brenda said, laughing, "Did y'all see me give that cutie that lap dance?" "Oh, God," Michelle said "Shell, don't listen to her, Girl. That's why she's still stayin' with my mother, always broke, 'cause she *gives* it away. And I'm livin' in my own condo, and payin' no bills. But, it looks like you handled Aaron just right tonight, Shell, 'cause he sure wants to see you again, Girlfriend. Listen to me, and do what I tell ya' and you won't have to worry about anything either", Michelle said, still teaching me how to get over.

Chapter 8

I heard someone knocking at the door. I wasn't expecting anyone, because Michelle and Aaron were both working, and they, and Arthur, Aaron's driver, were the only ones that ever came by Ms. Winston's to see me or pick me up. I peeped out the window beside the door and saw that it was Jerome. *I don't believe this! What is he doin' here?* I thought , because I hadn't seen him for almost a year. He looked just like he smelled, and that was b-a-a-d! I wondered, *When was the last time he took a shower?* I opened the door, slightly, and he said, "Hey, Brown Suga', how ya' doin'? Heard you were stayin' here, and I just had to see ya'. I've really missed ya'. I know you missed me too." Under my breath, I said to myself, *I don't think so!* "Ya' gonna' let me in?" "Naw, I was just getting' ready to go out." "Um-um-um, you sure look good, Baby. Where ya' goin'?" he asked, as if he had the right to. "Excuse me?" I said sarcastically. "I heard you been runnin' with Michelle and her wild sister. If y'all not doin' anything next week, I'm workin' a party for Miss Catherine's kid who's turnin' 21. Why don't y'all stop by?" "I'll see," I said, a little cocky, because I felt I had gone so far beyond him in maturity and lifestyle. "I'll look for ya' there," he said, leaning in and trying to kiss me on the cheek. "Jerome, don't even try it," I told him defiantly. "Aw, it's like *that*?" he asked. "Yeah, it's like *that*," I answered, confidently. "OK, Miss Thang. I'll look for ya' at the party," he said, and then he left.

Over the past year or so, I had learned more about life than the average person does, maybe in an *entire* lifetime. I had been schooled in the ways of the world by my friend, Michelle, who really became like a big sister to me, if you could call her that. She taught me "The Game"—how to *thrive*, not just survive, and I wanted that life! Take for instance, Aaron. He took me to the finest restaurants in town, wined and dined me, and after the evening was over, he always left me money on the night stand. (Sound familiar? Wonder what Jackie would call me – a prostitute? a ho'?) He made me feel so-o-o good! And I knew how to keep him coming back. He took me to the best hotels, and bought me the finest clothes and lingerie.

I remember the first time we went out together. The doorbell rang, and there, parked in front of my house, was a long, black stretch limo. The gentleman at the door said, "Miss MacDonald, my name is Arnold. Mr. Copeland sent me to pick you up." "Mr. Copeland? Who's Mr. Copeland?" I asked, confused. "Aaron Copeland, ma'am. I'm sorry. I should have explained," he answered. "Oh, *Aaron*," I said. "He also told me to give you this and to ask you if you would wear it tonight for him," Arnold said handing me a large box with a red ribbon wrapped around it. "I'll just be waiting outside in the car for you, ma'am." I ran into the house, and tore off that ribbon like a kid at Christmas tearing open her gift boxes.

When I opened the box, there was one long-stemmed rose on top of a bright red silk evening dress. The fragrance of the rose filled the room immediately. I ran to find a vase to put it in. Then I took the dress out of the box, and held it close to my body, as I looked in the mirror. I started dancing with it, like Cinderella at the ball. The dress came just above my knees, and it had a halter-like top that accentuated my breasts, and revealed my back. There were also matching shoes and a matching purse, topped off by a beautiful brooch with red and crystal inlays, and matching earrings. I thought, *Michelle was right. This is really livin'.* If Jerome only knew. What can someone like him *possibly* offer me now? And that's the way Aaron always treated me when we met, at least three times a week. We also stayed in the penthouse suite, wherever we went, like at the Palace Resort and Casino. The bellmen and all the hotel staff, including the manager, knew Aaron and treated him with the highest level of respect. He was a high roller and everybody knew it. And that turned me on. We developed an understanding about our relationship, which was that there were no ties, and that this was not an emotional love thing. We simply enjoyed each other during our times together, with no strings attached. I never had his phone number, and always wondered, in the back of my mind, why that was the case, though I somehow knew not to ask him. I did ask Michelle, and she explained, "That's just the rules of The Game, Shell. And as long as you're gettin' what you want, and *then* some, just relax. As my mother always said, use what ya' got to get what you want."

That following Saturday was the night Jerome was to DJ at the party he told me about. Aaron was out of town, and Michelle was away on vacation with Christian. I started getting restless, and before I knew it, I was getting dressed to go to the party. I put on some form-fitting black, Jordache jeans, my black Bandolino stiletto boots , a sparkling gold tank top, and my favorite cowboy hat, all the rage in 1984. I was so fine, I blew a kiss to *myself* in the mirror! I thought, *Girl, you know it's a shame to look this good!* And I realized, at that moment, that I wanted Jerome to regret the day he treated me badly as soon as he saw me looking this good when I walked in the door, because I wanted to gloat! I wanted to yell to him, "How ya' like me now? And ain't you sorry now that you cain't touch *this*?" "I'm just goin' over to Randall to help this kid celebrate turnin' 21, Ms. Winston. I won't be gone long," I yelled as I was leaving Ms. Winston's house. "OK, Shelley, Baby. I'll be right here when you get back," she answered. I hadn't seen Ms. Winston in a while because a good deal of the time, I stayed at Michelle's place. As for Momma, the only time I saw her was when I went over to The Gardens, against everyone's advice, but she didn't even recognize me. So I just let that go, and somehow found some peace with that, at least I thought I had.

When I got out of my taxi and walked in the door at the party, Cameo's *"She's Strange"* was pumping loud enough to be heard all down the street. The house was packed with wall-to-wall people, some dancing, some talking, and some just standing. But everyone was drinking wine coolers, because Rodney, Ms. Catherine's son, was now 21 years old, so the drinks flowed like water. Jerome was on the mike, scratching records and playing mixes. A lot of people whom I hadn't seen for a long time came over to me, telling me how good I looked and saying they were glad to see me. All eyes were on *me*, just like I had planned. When Jerome saw me, he waved Andre over to take over the DJ table. "Hey, Brown Suga'. Ya' look beautiful," Jerome said, trying to hug me, as I pushed him back. "Can we go someplace and talk?" "Naw, I'm not stayin' long," I told him, with complete detachment. "Well, let me at least get ya' a drink. Here," he said, handing me a wine cooler. "C'mon, let me introduce you to Ms. Catherine. It's her boy, Rodney who just had his 21st birthday." "Hi, Shelley. Jerome's told me so much about you. Make yourself at home," Ms. Catherine said warmly. "Thanks, but I can't stay long." Then Jerome took my hand and led me to the dance floor. He stuck to me like glue the rest of the party, and I was drinking wine coolers as if they were Kool-Aid. Finally, I said good-bye to everyone, as I was feeling a little tipsy from the wine. "Hold up, Brown Suga'. I'll take ya' home," Jerome said. "Look, I ain't your Brown Suga', so you need to stop calling me that. My name is Shelley!" I said caustically. "My bad, Shelley. Now, may I take you home?" "OK," I answered, too light-headed to protest. He drove me to Ms. Winston's house, and, because I was feeling a little dizzy, he followed me to the basement. Then he helped me undress and began kissing me, gently and slowly. Next, he kissed me on my neck, knowing that was my most vulnerable area, and proceeded to lay me on the bed and put me to sleep with his loving.

The next morning, when I found myself naked and reeking of alcohol, I remembered what had taken place. *Shelley, have you lost your mind? How could you stoop so low, when you've been living so high?* I berated myself. Then I heard the phone ring. For some reason, I let it ring three or four times, as if I already knew who was calling. "Hello, Shelley. How ya' feelin'," Jerome said, as if we were best friends again. "How am I feelin'? How do you think I'm feelin'? You took advantage of me 'cause I drank too much," I practically screamed at him. "Naw, Shelley, it wasn't like that." "It was *just* like that, so from now on, you forget this number, and don't darken my path ever again. Ya' got that?" And I slammed the phone receiver down so hard, it's a wonder I didn't break the phone. I was furious with Jerome, but also with myself and vowed that I'd never lose control like that again.

A couple of months after that, I had been feeling sick at the stomach, and had all the flu symptoms that everyone else was getting. Ms. Winston called the clinic and made an appointment for me with Dr. Simpson. I went to the appointment and came out with a prescription for antibiotics. When I got home, the phone was ringing and it was Dr. Simpson. "Miss MacDonald, have you filled that antibiotic prescription yet"? he asked.

"No, not yet. I was just gettin' ready to go to the drugstore when I heard the phone ring," I said, wondering why he had asked. "Good. Because I want you to tear up that prescription. Miss MacDonald, our tests indicate that you're about two months pregnant. And with that being the case, we don't want you to take any antibiotics. Now I want you to call my office and schedule an appointment so we can get you started on your vitamins and regular check ups with me. OK?" After a long sigh, I responded, "OK." When I hung up that phone, I screamed so loud, most people would have thought I was being beaten, which was appropriate, because I felt beat down. Just when my life was about to take off in a whole new direction, filled with an abundance of the *good* life, this had to happen. And what made it even more tragic was that I knew the father of this baby had to be *Jerome*. It couldn't have been Aaron, because we were always cautious and protected ourselves against that eventuality. How could I take care of a baby, living in a pit of a basement with pipes leaking, sleeping on a mattress on the floor, and using crate boxes as a dresser? And, even though this was more an occasional drop-in spot for me now, since I stayed at Michelle's condo most of the time, I knew that Michelle would not be likely to entertain bringing a baby to live there with us. But, since she was my best friend, I had to call her and tell her. With each ring of Michelle's phone, I repeatedly said to myself, *I can't believe this. Not again,* I lamented through oceans of tears. "Michelle. Are you sittin' down, Girl? You not gonna' believe this," I said after Michelle answered the phone. "What, Shell? What's goin' on?" "Girl," I said with a huge sigh.

"What, Shell? Just say it!" Michelle said anxiously. "Michelle, Girl. I'm pregnant," I said reluctantly. "You're what? How'd you let this happen? And Aaron, he knows The Game," Michelle said, getting ready to tear Aaron a brand new one. "Hold up, Girl. It's not Aaron's baby." I explained. "Oh n-o-o-o-o! Please don't tell me it's that sorry behind Jerome's baby! So what're you gonna' do?" she asked. "What do ya' mean, what am I gonna' do?" I said with affront. "Well, I'm sure if you come up with half the money and Jerome comes up with half, we can take care of this today at the clinic." "Girl, are you crazy? I ain't gettin' nobody's abortion. This is *my* baby. I'm not killin' *my* baby! I cain't turn my back on my own baby and abandon it, like I was abandoned!" I proclaimed, with resolve. "OK, Girl. It's yo' life. Well, look, I gotta' go, Shell. Call me if you need me," Michelle said, ending the conversation, with a tone of disappointment in *me* in her voice.

Over the next nine months, I only talked with Michelle a couple of times, and Aaron was an afterthought for the moment. Michelle told me that Christian had informed Aaron about my pregnancy, and, though he was reluctant to come and see me, he did call from time to time to see if I needed anything. He also left the door open for us to resume our relationship after the baby was born. When Ms. Winston got home that evening, I told her I was pregnant. "Well, Shelley. Ya' made your bed. Ya' gotta' lay in it. Tomorrow, we'll go down to the County Welfare office and get you set up for assistance, and we'll go to the clinic and get your appointments set up. Ya' know I'll do whatever I can for ya'."

I was shopping in the mall, one day, starting to buy things for the baby. All of a sudden, I heard, "Shelley, you pregnant? Is it mine?," he asked, excitedly. "Yes, it's yours, Jerome." And as I was finishing my sentence, he tried to draw me closer to him. "Look. If you want to be in this baby's life, you better get a steady job, and I don't mean spinnin' no records. I mean a job where you can help support this baby. But as for *us*, there is no *us* now, and there never will be *again*! You got that?" I said adamantly, as I was walking away from him. "Yeah, Shelley, I got it, I got it," Jerome said, quieter than I'd ever heard him.

"Ms. Winston, Ms. Winston! Come down here quickly! I'm peeing on myself and I cain't stop!" I yelled up from the basement. I was in my ninth month of pregnancy, just a few days from my projected delivery date. "Oh, my Lord, Shelley. Yo' water just broke. Here, put these towels in between your legs and let me help you put on some fresh panties. Let's hurry, 'cause you about to push this baby out, and I don't want you to do it in my car," Ms. Winston said truthfully. Then sharp pains hit my stomach like I'd never felt before. We reached the hospital in about 10 minutes, but it felt like hours, because the pains were coming so fast and furiously. I kept panting, as I held my stomach, and tried not to push, because every time I pushed, I felt like my insides were about to drop out. "Stop pushin', Shelley. It ain't time for that yet. Hold on. We're about there," Ms. Winston said, unable to disguise the panic in her voice. When we reached the hospital, they had already been alerted by my doctor that I was a high risk pregnancy, due to my age and Rh-negative blood type, so they rushed me to the maternity ward right away. When they examined me, I had already dilated almost five centimeters, and was screaming at the top of my lungs. Thank goodness, my baby was as impatient to be in this world, as I was to have him here. My son, Brandon, was born in 1.5 hours of my arriving at the hospital, weighing 7.5lbs, and was 20 inches long. He was a beautiful, healthy baby boy, and he was all *mine*. I had never felt so much love and pride about any-thing as I did about my baby Brandon. The next morning, as I held him, I was so overwhelmed with unbelievable passion and unabashed love for this child, that I felt com-pelled to say to him, as I held him, "Brandon, I will always love you and I'll always be there for you. I'll never leave you, because you're the most important thing in my life. Trust me."

As sweet tears were streaming down my face, just look-ing at my son, I heard, "Sweetheart, he is so gorgeous! My heart's burstin' for you 'cause from this moment on, your life will change forever. Now you'll be livin' not just for yourself, but for this precious blessin' that's been given to you. Scoot over a little bit so I can get in the bed with you and hug you both. Shelley, Baby, this is truly what love's all about," Jackie said, sliding in the bed with us. And she hugged us and rocked us both, while she hummed a song that, again, sounded so familiar to me, even though I *still* didn't know why that was so.

Jerome came around every now and then to see Brandon, but he always came empty-handed, with the stench of alcohol still lingering over his whole body. When he *did* bring anything, it was from his mother, not from him. After a few months of this, I cut him off completely from Brandon's life, because I knew he would never be a daddy to Brandon, because of the path he chose to take in his *own* life.

I was grocery shopping, and Brandon was riding in the baby seat of the grocery cart, when a lady came up to me and said, "Hi, Shelley. I haven't seen you since you had the baby, but, I gotta' tell you, you sure are lookin' good for someone who recently had a baby." I recognized, a moment later, that it was Ms. Catherine, whom I had met at that ill-fated party. Then she hugged me and kissed me, affectionately, on the cheek. "And is this handsome young man, Brandon? Shelley, he's just adorable! Hello, Precious," she said, stroking Brandon's cheek and smiling at him. Brandon smiled back with the sweetest and broadest smile he could muster. He looked so cute. He had always been such a *good* baby, and he was never afraid of people, even those he'd never seen. "Oh, Shelley. I could just eat those fat jaws up," Ms. Catherine gushed. "Now, Jerome told me that you and your baby are still stayin' in a basement in Templeton. Is that right, Shelley?" she asked. "Yes, ma'am. We're stayin' with Ms. Winston until I can afford somethin' better." "Well, I guess it was just meant for us to run into each other today, so I could tell you that with my son gone, I've got a lot of room in my house. Just me and my daughter, Tanya, are there now, and there'd be plenty of room for you and little Brandon, there. Plus, Shelley, you can have your own large room and bathroom, and I wouldn't charge you anymore than you're payin' right now. I'd feel so much better if you and the baby moved back to Randall, and no longer had to stay in Templeton, 'cause that ain't no place for a young girl like you to be by yourself, let alone raisin' a baby. So what do you think, Shelley? You can move in today, if you want to. We can go now and get your things and me and Tanya will help you move them in." It must have taken me all of two minutes to tell her, "Thanks, Ms. Catherine. I really appreciate it, 'cause I've been wantin' to get out of that basement ever since Brandon was born. It's just too dark and damp, and I don't want him to get sick. Why don't I do this. Ms Winston has been very kind to me and Brandon, so I don't just want to up and leave her. I want to tell her first, so why don't I move to your place on Saturday? Could you and Tanya still help me move on Saturday?" "Then Saturday it is, Shelley. We'll pick you up about 10:00 in the morning. OK? Oh, I just can't wait to have a baby in the house again, since my youngest baby, Tanya, is already a teenager. This is just goin' to be wonderful," Ms. Catherine declared with a great deal of exuberance and certainty. "Oh! One more thing, Ms. Catherine. You need to know that even though Jerome is the father of my baby, he ain't done one thing for this baby, so I've removed him from Brandon's life. I'm tellin' you that 'cause I don't want you to let him near my baby, in my absence. OK?" "I completely understand, Shelley. And, as a matter of fact, I always wondered why you were even with Jerome in the first place, because you could do so much better than him." Ms. Catherine said with conviction. "I know that now. And he is truly now a thing of the past for me, Ms. Catherine. I've finally gotten him out of my life!" I almost yelled. We both laughed. Then she hugged me again and told me she'd see me on Saturday.

When I told Ms. Winston I would be moving, though she was sad to be losing her Little Man, Brandon, she was happy that we'd be living in a better environment. So we moved back to Randall in Ms. Catherine's house, and we became one big, happy family. Ms. Catherine treated me like I was a girlfriend more than a daughter, probably because I was mature for my age. I was only 15 years old, but had lived the life of women at least 10+ years older than me. And while she was closer to my mother's age, Ms. Catherine still felt an affinity with me. Actually, we began to smoke weed together, along with her daughter, Tanya, and would sometimes go out together. Tanya was crazy about my baby, Brandon, and would babysit with him any time I needed her to. I really was looking and feeling as good as I was when I ran around with Michelle and Brenda, but I was starting to resent the fact that I had so little money, just living off Assistance. Catherine, which is what she insisted that I call her now, instead of *Miss* Catherine, patiently listened to my complaints about not having enough money, and she'd always respond, "Just wait, Shelley. We'll figure somethin' out."

I'll never forget the day she figured something out. We had finished dinner, and were smoking our third joint, when she said, "Shelley. What if I told you that I know a way we can make some money fast?" "What you talkin' about, Catherine? How much money?" I asked, intrigued and curious. "A lot of money. Say, $10,000 for you alone." "Ten thousand dollars? What do we have to do, *kill* somebody?" I yelled in disbelief. "Listen. I know this white guy who is a vice-president of his company. I met him one time at the riverboat casino, and we got to know each other pretty well, because we both like to play Black Jack, and go to the casinos all the time. His name is Walter Hopkins. He always had so much money to gamble with that one time I was just bold enough to ask him what he did and where he'd gotten all his money. He was so drunk, like he usually is, that he told me it's the money from his company that he deposits every Friday night. But, before he makes the drop, he stops and gambles trying to double the amount, so he can take home the winnings he got, using the company's money to gamble, as long as he replaces and deposits that money." I sat there listening, totally enthralled. "Then I said to him, you carry around this much money cash on you every Friday? And he had the nerve to tell me, yes! Another thing I found out is that he likes young, brown-skinned girls, 'cause he asked me one time if I knew any. Now, Shelley, I told him that I did know a pretty young brown-skinned girl, and you were the person I immediately thought of. So here's the plan. Tomorrow is Friday, the day he has all the drop money. I already arranged with him that I would have you meet him at the Clover Hotel around 8:00 p.m. before he goes to the casino. Now, you don't have to sleep with him, Shelley. But just make sure he takes all his clothes off. Because, what's gonna' happen is that my good friend Willie is gonna' start bangin' on the hotel door, sayin' you his daughter and he's gonna' call the cops if you don't come out of the room. And we think Walter will be so scared, that when Willie comes in that room acting like he's gonna' beat him, with bat in hand, and demands money from him to keep from callin' the cops, he'll definitely hand over the money. And if he doesn't do it willingly, Willie knows where to look for it. So, are you down are not, Shelley?" Catherine asked me. "Ten thousand dollars just for me? And I don't have to sleep with this ol' fart? Yeah, I'm in," I said, tired of the desperation I always felt because I had to scramble for money.

Friday night, I was driven to the hotel as planned. Catherine waited in the car outside. I knocked on the door, and Walter quickly let me in. This was the oldest, white man I think I'd ever seen. Every inch of his body was wrinkled and red. I thought, *You got to be crazy if you think you can touch this!* I quickly said, "Hi, Walter. My name is Shelley. Listen. I'm gonna' freshen up a bit in the bathroom, and when I get back, I wanna' see you relaxed on the bed. OK?" "You're so beautiful, Shelley. Don't take long." he said, looking like some fiendish character from a sci-fi movie.

When I got in the bathroom, it was all I could do to keep from throwing up, not from fear, just from disgust. As if the sight of him alone wasn't enough to gag me, as I proceeded into the bathroom, I saw the bathroom walls covered with pictures of young, brown-skinned girls posed spread eagle. I rationalized to myself, *You ol', perverted freak! You deserve everything that's goin' down tonight.* I stayed in the bathroom as long as I could, when I heard him say, "Shelley, I'm waiting." I stayed fully dressed, opened the door to the bathroom and walked toward the bed, where I saw that this old geezer had outfitted himself in black leather S&M attire. I couldn't believe it! "C'mon over here, Beauty. Let me take your clothes off," he said slurring.

Bang! Bang! Bang! "Open this door!" we both heard. Walter bolted up on the bed and turned as white as a sheet. "Open this door right now or I'll call the police. You got my daughter in there! Shelley, Baby, you alright?" Willie yelled. "Yeah, Daddy, I'm OK," I yelled as I went to open the door. Walter scrambled to get his clothes on, blanched white with trepidation. When I opened the door, Willie bounded in with a bat in his hand, screaming, "I oughtta' break yo' knees right here and now, before I call the police. You got my daughter here. Do you know how old she is? Man, I could kill you, and no one would put me in jail," Willie threatened. "Wait a minute, wait a minute," Walter pleaded in total fear. "I got money. Just take it and go." "You think I'd take yo' chump change when I know what you were gonna' do to my daughter?" "No, no. It's not chump change. Here, look!" Walter said, pulling the money from his blazer and spreading it on the bed. "How much is this?" Willie demanded. "There's sixty-five thousand dollars right here. Take it all and go. Please!" Walter begged. Then Willie grabbed up the money, put it back in the large envelope it had come in, and motioned for me to follow him out of the room. "You damned lucky you had this much money on you, 'cause you might be dead right now, if you didn't have it. From now on, you best be careful who you messin' with," Willie chided him. Then we rushed to the car and drove away with Catherine. All the way home, we laughed hysterically. And when we got home, we threw the money on the dining room table, lit up some joints and laughed all night long about that 'ol fool whose depraved perversions had finally caught up with him.

But apparently the joke was on *us*! About 6:00 a.m., we heard a knock on the door, and someone shouted, "Open up! It's the police!" Tanya was the first person up and she opened the door. "Is there a Catherine and Shelley that live here?" the officer asked firmly. "Yes sir," Tanya answered. Catherine came in the room and said, "What's goin' on?" Tanya came and got me out of my room, and as I was carrying Brandon in my arms, the police officer said to Catherine, "Is your name Catherine?" "Yes," she answered, meekly. "And I guess you're Shelley?" "Yes, sir," I answered, scared stiff. "You're both under arrest for robbery." Tanya took Brandon from my arms and they handcuffed us both, as they read us our rights. Catherine was taken to the County Jail, and I was taken to Juvenile Detention, but not before being fingerprinted and photographed. I contacted Michelle when I got to Juvenile Detention and told her what had happened. She couldn't believe it, but she told me she'd do all she could to help me get out. I was also almost spastic because I was worried about Brandon, and Michelle said she'd go over and get him, so I didn't have to worry about him. That first night in Juvey, I was as frightened as I've ever been in my life. It was cold and dark, and you could hear girls screaming from their cells, "New girl in the house! New girl in the house!" I was glad to be in a cell by myself, left alone to cry all night long.

"Shelley MacDonald. Is this really you? What're you doin' here? What got you to risk so much of your life? To risk your freedom?, Jackie asked. "Lord, Lord, Lord, Shelley. Why do you insist on takin' the long way around to havin' the life that you're destined to live? You think about that, Shelley. Think about why you keep ridin' this train of destruction. Open yo' eyes, Baby, before it's too late." Jackie said. I couldn't answer her, because I was too drained and too despondent. "Alright, come here. Let me get my hug, 'cause you know I love you, even though I don't like how you're livin' your life."

"I'm sorry, Jackie," I said sincerely. "I *know* you are, especially windin' up in a place like *this*." Jackie held me for a while until I finally drifted off to sleep.

After three days of detainment, to my surprise, I was suddenly released with all charges dropped, and Michelle came and picked me up. As it turned out, Walter had dropped all charges against me, because he didn't want charges brought against *him* for soliciting a minor. As far as Catherine's and Willie's fates? They both had to remain in jail to face charges for robbery. When I saw Brandon in Michelle's arms, I grabbed him and kissed him a thousand times on his chubby cheeks. It was as if I had been away from him forever, and he must have felt the same way, because he immediately reached out for me when he saw me. "Shell, Girl, this is one crazy mess you got yourself into. That was not The Game I taught you. What were you thinking?" Michelle asked, making me feel two feet tall. "That's just it. I *wasn't* thinking." "Obviously!" Michelle said, with a hint of censure in her tone. "Well, on a lighter note, Aaron's been askin' about you a lot. Are you ready to start livin' the good life agin?" "Girl, yes. I thought you'd never ask!" I eagerly declared. So Michelle moved Brandon and me to live with her in her condo until I could move on my own. I was back where I belonged.

Chapter 9

"C'mon, Brandon, Baby. Let's go see Grandma Winston," I said to my baby as we walked out of the house to Michelle's car. Every weekend, Brandon went to spend the weekend with Ms. Winston, who had really become a surrogate grandmother to him. After we dropped him off, Michelle and I headed to *Escape*. Brenda, Michelle's sister, was going to meet us there later. "Now look, Shell. Keep your mouth shut. You can't tell all your business, 'cause nobody knows anything about this whole incident, not even Christian. They just know that you had a baby, and that's why they hadn't seen you for a while. And that's all they need to know. Ya' feel me?" "No problem, Michelle. I won't mess up this time," I said with absolutely no doubt in my mind that I was telling the truth.

"Hey, Shell, long time no see," Reuben greeted me, by giving me a big hug. "Hey, Reuben, I've missed you *too*," I said enthusiastically. "Well, don't be such a stranger again, Shell," Reuben said opening the door to the club for us.

When we got up to the VIP Lounge, there were a few new faces in the group that I didn't recognize. The old crew members all came up to me and hugged me, welcoming me back. Then, I spotted Aaron, who was making his way toward me, looking as clean as the Board of Health! "Hey, Baby. It's good to see you. Always looking beautiful, as usual," he said, kissing me on the cheek. "Aaron, Baby, introduce me to your friend," this very attractive, young woman said to him, as she grabbed his arm. *Baby? Did I just hear her call Aaron Baby? I wonder who she thinks she is*? I wondered, feeling indignant, as I drew back, looking her up and down. Michelle walked up just then, having seen my body language, and whispered in a voice low enough that no one else could hear her but me, "Chill, Girl. You been gone a long time. OK? Things change." Catching her drift, I regained my composure, when I heard Aaron say, "Baby, this is an old friend of mine, Shell. Shell this is Judy." So we exchanged pleasantries, and I sat down next to Michelle, sipping a glass of champagne, curious about what the evening would bring next.

After a while, Aaron began walking toward me, bringing with him one of the finest specimens of God's creation of man that I'd ever seen! Jet black curly hair adorned his head like a crown. His mocha-hued skin was as smooth as a baby's behind. The irises in his eyes looked like black onyx, surrounded by the whitest and purest mother of pearl. His smile revealed perfectly symmetrical, brilliant white teeth. I thought, *I bet his breath smells fresh too*, remembering what Jackie had told me, sometime ago about only accepting a man with a fresh mouth and fresh breath. Then, there was that body, ripped over a six foot two inch frame, as if he were the world's best personal fitness trainer. And covering all that pulchritude was a black, form-fitting shirt that accentuated all of his positives, black pants and a black jacket, designed by Armani, of course, and black, highly polished leather loafers. His walk was as sensuous as he looked; gliding toward me as though he were moving in slow motion, with that sexy, sumptuous Denzel Washington walk that makes women of all ages wanna' holla'! The Greek Adonis didn't have anything on *this* brother!

"Shell, I wanna' introduce you to my, boy, Kev, from D.C. Kev, this is the lovely Shell." "And lovely she is," Kev responded flashing all 32's. I was thinking, *You so fine, Baby, I wouldn't mind havin' yo' baby!* He opened his mouth and said in the deepest, sexiest voice, "Shell, would you like to..." and before he could get *dance* out of his mouth, I said, "Yes," eagerly awaiting the bliss that I knew awaited me. Kev chuckled slightly and led me to the dance floor. We were never apart that night, from that moment on. "What're your plans for the rest of the night," Kev asked, as it was nearing time for the club to close. "Whatever your plans are," I answered, boldly.

"Let's get outta' here, then. I'm staying at the Ritz up the street. Let's call room service and top off the night with some appetizers and wine. How's that sound?" "Like heaven," I said, with no hesitation. Kev said our good-byes to the crew, and as I looked over at Michelle, who was sitting on Christian's lap, she gave me a subtle thumbs up.

The valet pulled up in a brand new, 1985 black Mercedes Benz with camel leather interior, and a mahogany dashboard. Kev opened the passenger door for me, and I felt like my fifteen minutes of fame were happening right at that moment! All eyes were on us, and I knew we made a striking couple. Kev was in the Executive Penthouse, of course, and I wasn't surprised by that. He told me to make myself comfortable, as he turned on soft background music, and phoned Room Service. He took off his jacket and shirt, exposing that body with its washboard abs, huge biceps, ripped ribcage and broad shoulders that seemed to go on forever. Then he put on a smoking jacket, leaving it open for me to salivate as I stripped him naked with my eyes. And he knew exactly what he was doing, which, I've got to admit, worked liked a charm. Because Sistah Girl, here, was getting so turned on, I had to go to the bathroom. As soon as I closed and locked the bathroom door, I squealed, "YES-S-S-S!," jumping up and down with pure glee.

"Shell, is everything alright?" Kev inquired, having apparently heard my not so subtle exclamation of joy. "Yes it is, Kev. I'll be out in a moment," I said, after clearing my throat. Then, after examining myself again in the mirror, I opened the bathroom door. Kev was standing there, waiting for me, with a glass of Cristal champagne. We sat down, made small talk, and started kissing passionately while we explored each other's body with our hands. We were almost at the boiling point, when there was a knock on the door. "Room Service," they announced. Reluctantly, Kev got up, saying, "'Excuse me, Baby. This'll just take a minute. Don't lose that thought!" When he returned, I had positioned myself on the bed in the most seductive pose I could summon.

When he walked back in the room, he just stood there, looking me up and down, with that matchless smile flashed across his face. Then he leaned down and opened a duffel bag that was lying beside the bed, and pulled out what looked like a white, shredded T-shirt. "I want to play a game with you, Shell." "What kinda game?" I asked "Just trust me," he said calmly. "Don't worry. I'll be gentle." I began to feel a little uneasy and somewhat suspicious, but I didn't want to jump to conclusions and ruin what had been a magical night, up to now. So I went along with the program. Then he tied my hands above my head through the design spaces on the headboard, and bound my feet together. When he did that, my fear started elevating and I was getting more than just a little alarmed. Next, he started kissing me on my feet, working his way up my legs to my belly button and my breasts. To be truthful, that felt so good that I started to relax, and my fear began to subside. Then, what did he do but go to the most erogenous and vulnerable area of my body, my neck, and started kissing all around my neck. I began to tingle with excitement, fantasizing about the absolute pleasure he would give me. Soft caresses with his hands on my neck, followed. Soon, I was on fire, ever so ready to feel his manhood inside of me. I had not had a man from the time I learned I was pregnant, up until now, so my hormones were raging out of control.

Suddenly, I felt pressure on my neck, which brought me back to reality. "Kev, I can't breathe, Baby. You're squeezing my neck too hard." Kev did not respond verbally. Instead the pressure became greater on my neck to the point where I could barely breathe at all, and he seemed to be *enjoying* it. At this point, I started struggling, trying to get him off of me. When I looked in his face, what I saw there made me terror-stricken. His eyes were glazed over as if he were in a trance. That brilliant smile became the sinister scowl of a mad man committing the most horrid act of sadism, yet unable to stop his demented obsession until the act was done. Kev was breathing harder with each added pressure of his hands to my throat, as if he were a man reaching an orgasm. When we first got to the hotel it was raining outside, but as it became harder and harder for me to breathe, the sound of the raindrops became more and more distant, until, finally, I couldn't hear them at all. I had blacked out completely.

As I regained consciousness, I looked over to my left, and saw Kev was sound asleep. I tried to get up from the bed, but was still restrained because my hands were still tied to the headboard. Slowly, I bent my knees, and twisted my body around to the point where I could get up on my knees. Luckily, the knots in the restraints were tied loosely, so I used my teeth and started untying each strip, one at a time. Every time Kev turned over, I froze like a block of ice. But he was still in deep sleep. It didn't take me long to completely free my hands. Then, I untied my bound feet in a matter of minutes. The room was pitch dark, and I could barely see, but I grabbed whatever clothes I could find, plus my purse, and quickly, and ever so quietly, slipped out the front door of the suite. I ran, half-dressed, as fast as I could and went down the stairs to street level. There was a phone booth at the corner and I ran there barefoot, hoping no one would see me. It was still pouring down rain, and I was completely soaked by the time I reached the phone booth. Shaking like a leaf, and still terrified Kev might wake up and come looking for me, I could barely get the coins out of my bag to put in the phone.

I don't know how much money I dropped on the floor of the phone booth before I finally stopped trembling enough to deposit enough money in the phone. I dialed Michelle's number, and it seemed to ring and ring forever. "Michelle, please be home. Please pick up the phone!" "Hel-l-o-o," Michelle answered, "Christian, Baby, what could you want at this hour? I know you ain't even tryin' to make this a booty call at 3:00 a.m. in the mornin'." Michelle said, still groggy with sleep. "Michelle, it's Shelley. Come and get me," I said in a hoarse, gravelly voice, a result of the near-strangulation I had been through. "Come and get you? Girl, come and get you from where? What's goin' on?" "Look, come and get me. I'm in a phone booth on a corner across the street from the Ritz Hotel. I'll give you the details later. But Kev tried to *kill* me." "What? He tried to *kill* you?" "Yes, Michelle. I'll tell you about it when you get here. Please hurry!" "OK, OK. I'll be right there." I knew it would take Michelle at least a half hour to get there, maybe longer in the rain. I was scared to death that Kev might wake up and come looking for me, so I opened the door of the phone booth just enough so the light would go out, and squatted down in the phone booth so no one could see me. Lo and behold, I had just squatted down when I saw Kev driving that black Mercedes Benz slowly down the street, as he looked from one side of the street to the other.

"Don't worry, Baby. He won't see you. I've fixed his eyes so he wouldn't even see you if you were standin' in the light." Jackie said. She was standing in the rain right in front of the door to the phone booth. And, even though it was pouring outside, she was dry as a bone. When I saw her, I instantly jumped up in her arms and clung to her like my life depended on it, crying frantically. "There, there, now. I'm here, my Shelley. And right after you blacked out, I made sure that *he* blacked out, or he would have snuffed out this life of yours that holds so much promise. It just wasn't your time to go, Suga', and this time, I stepped in, touched him like he touched you, and made him black out too! Now I'm gonna' give you this lotion to rub your neck with, and in a little while, you won't even see his finger marks on your neck anymore, like you do now. But the marks I gave him on his neck, he'll never be able to get rid of. So just rest here while I hold you 'til Michelle gets here. You won't be bothered by his kind no more. Trust me." And I did.

Just before Michelle pulled up, about a half hour later, Jackie was gone. When I told Michelle what happened with Kev she was so mad she wanted to call Aaron and Christian as soon as we got home and tell them about Aaron's *boy*. I begged her not to because I really wanted to put this nightmare out of my mind forever. Then Michelle said something that registered deeply with me. She said, "You know, Shell. I really don't think life in The Game is for *you*." "Why do you say that, Michelle? I didn't do anything wrong did I?" "No, Little Sis. It wasn't *you*. But sometimes in The Game, we never know who's gonna' break the rules. And what Kev did to you is the extreme of breakin' the rules. And because we never know who's gonna' cheat, that's the risk of playin' The Game. But now that you have that sweet baby of yours, Brandon, in there, these are risks I won't let you take anymore. You understand what I'm sayin', Shell?" Michelle said with more concern and more conviction than I'd ever heard from her.

"Yeah, I guess," I answered, still not completely convinced that I should be out of The Game altogether. But, what I *did* understand was that I needed to get a job soon, so I could get a place of my own for me and my baby. I went to bed that night determined to start an earnest job hunt as soon as possible.

That next morning, I was searching through the papers, trying to find a job that I knew I could do. Michelle walked into the kitchen, peeped over my shoulder and said, "You lookin' for a job, Shell?" "Yeah, Michelle. You know I can't stay here with you forever. I gotta' find a job so me and Brandon can get a place of our own." "Do you remember Ms. Johnston who owns that fine dining restaurant Christian and Aaron took us to just over the county line, Antoinette's House of Southern Cuisine?" I nodded that I remembered her.

What I remembered was that Ms. Johnston was an elegant, strikingly beautiful Creole lady from Louisiana who owned one of the most upscale restaurants in the Randall area. The service was of the highest quality and the food was exquisite. She had studied to be a chef at one of the finest schools in Paris, France, and, after years of working in fine dining restaurants, became the owner of her very own four star restaurant.

"Well she's one of my regular clients, and she's always complaining about being short-staffed. I'll ask her if she has any openings and I'll see if I can get you hooked up with her. OK?" "Thanks, Michelle. I don't know what I'd do without you." "Aw, you know you my Girl, Shell. And I'm gonna' always look out for you." "Ms. Winston already told me that she'd babysit for me, when I start working, so that's already arranged," I informed Michelle. "Good. Then I'll call Ms. Johnston today, and try to get you set up to see her." Sure enough, Michelle got me an appointment with Mrs. Johnston the very next day. She hired me on the spot to work in her restaurant. I started to work the next day after I was hired.

A few days later, Michelle called me at the restaurant. "Shell, quick! Turn on Channel 6!" she yelled. "What? What's goin' on, Michelle?" "Just turn it on, and you'll see!" she insisted. I reached up and punched the channel button to Channel 6, turning up the volume slightly. There, blasted on TV, was a mug shot of a black man named

Terence Binford. The reporter was saying that this Terence Binford had been captured after having been wanted for questioning in several states for the unsolved deaths by strangulation of six young women. When I looked more closely at his face, there was no doubt in my mind that it was the "Kev" who had almost strangled me the other night at the Ritz. The reporter went on to say, "Terence Binford made the critical mistake of thinking that he was untouchable. But when he killed Alexis Fisher here at the Ritz Hotel last night, who was discovered by a housekeeper, he made the fatal error of leaving his DNA tracks on her body. He was apprehended at 3:00 p.m. this afternoon due to an all points bulletin alert that described his car and license plate number, which had been obtained from hotel records. Another compelling mystery about this man is that when the police apprehended him, on *his* neck were deep finger marks that went around *his* neck, as if someone had attempted to strangle *him* also. But since he won't talk to the authorities, we have no clue how those marks got on *his* neck. We can only speculate that one of his victims tried to fight back. Terence Binford had many aliases, and was using the name of Kevin Taylor when he registered here at the Ritz. The hotel management stated that just a few nights ago, he had entertained another young woman in his hotel suite. There is no word or indication who she was, or if she is still alive. Terence Binford has refused to talk at all to authorities. We'll continue to bring you updates as this case proceeds. This has been Channel 6 Late Breaking News, live at the Ritz Hotel. Rob Singleton reporting." I ran to the bathroom feeling sick to my stomach. I actually vomited so much, that I felt like my insides were coming out. *Jackie had said that he would have permanent marks on his neck and he has them, just like she said. But Oh God, please forgive me. Why didn't I report this animal to the police? Why? If I had, would this girl's life have been spared?* I asked myself, wracked with guilt and shame. To this day, I still wonder.

Chapter 10

My life took a completely different turn, after that life-threatening incident with Kev, or Terence Binford, or whatever his name was. I was determined to get myself together so I could get a place for Brandon and me, and I made him the major focus in my life. I stopped going to *Escape* with Michelle, because I didn't want to be tempted by the bling-bling that might, once again, turn out to be tarnished brass, rather than the pure gold it was purported to be. I started saving my money and located exactly where I wanted to move. Michelle still made Brandon and me welcome in her home, and she refused to accept any money from me for rent. She was also happy to see that I had accepted, to some degree, the fact that this was not the time for me to be involved in The Game. In fact, she later told me that I should never be involved, ever again. So, I turned my attention to being the best waitress at work, and to being the best mother to my baby boy. I worked as many hours as I could, and soon started accumulating enough money to move.

Ms. Johnston, the owner of the restaurant, took me under her wing, because she liked me and liked my spunk, as she called it. She said I reminded her of herself, when she was young, because she too, had been a young mother who had to make a way for herself and her daughter without the help of her daughter's father. And even though I had lied when I interviewed for the job, saying I was 18 rather than the 15.5 years old that I actually was at the time, I believe she really knew I wasn't 18 when she hired me. She never confirmed that with me, because the subject of my age never came up again, but I just know she knew somehow. Ms. Johnston began teaching me the management end of the business, and, before long, made me her right hand, promoting me to Assistant Manager. That increase in pay gave me what I needed to move into my own place.

I was so proud and happy the day Brandon and I moved. I had leased a three-bedroom row house in the city. It was in a decent neighborhood, and on the bus line, so Brandon and I could get wherever we needed to go on the bus. Ms. Winston had retired, and became Brandon's full-time babysitter. And, yes. she had completely stopped using any drugs and had been drug-free for sometime before I let her keep Brandon from the very beginning. She came and picked him up in the morning, dropped me off at the restaurant, and took him to her home the rest of the day. Even when I had to work overtime, I didn't have to worry about my baby, because I knew he was in good hands. I furnished my place with second-hand furniture, and used crates as tables, at first, but that didn't matter. This was *my* place, and I felt a sense of accomplishment with this new-found independence that I had never felt before in my life.

"Hey Shelley. Come here a minute. I want you to meet somebody," Ted Swats said as I was walking past his booth in the more secluded area of the restaurant. Ted was a regular at the restaurant, and he usually had an entourage of people with him whenever he came.

"I'll be right there, Ted. Just give me a second," I said. Ted was always introducing me to someone, as if he had taken it upon himself as his life's mission to hook me up with someone of his own choosing, since he had never gotten to first base with me in all the times he had asked me out. "Shelley, this is my homeboy Dimitri Toliver. He just moved here from Chicago a few months ago, and I've had a hard time trackin' 'im down, he's so busy, but I finally did today. And, ya' know I had ta' bring him to my favorite place ta' be to meet one of my favorite people. Right?" "Nice to meet you, Mr. Toliver. I hope you'll enjoy living here. It really is a nice community. Now what are you drinking? It's on the house as our way of saying welcome to Antoinette's," I said, always the consummate, customer service-oriented manager. "I'd love a glass of Moet champagne if you have any, Shelley? Right?" "That's right, and Moet it'll be, Mr. Toliver. Ted, what can I get *you*?" "Shell, why don't you just bring us a couple of bottles of Moet and glasses for everybody so we can celebrate my boy's move here. OK, Sweet Thang?" "That's an excellent idea, Ted. Shall I run your usual tab? Mr. Toliver, that first glass is still on the house for *you*." "And what about *me*, your best customer? Don't I deserve a glass on the house?" Ted said half-serious, half-joking. "Ted, when you leave Randall and then come back here one day to live, we'll gladly celebrate your homecoming by giving you a glass of Moet on the house, but, we've given you so many in the past, already, that I think *this* time we'll add it to your tab, Love. OK?" I said sweetly but confidently, as everyone at the table exploded in laughter, including Ted. "I'll send Janisse over with your Moet shortly, and she'll take the rest of your order. Very good meeting you, Mr. Toliver," I said as I walked away from the table. "Dimitri. Please call me Dimitri," Ted's friend said as I was walking away. "Dimitri," I said in my sultry, chanteuse-like voice, looking back at him. "R-i-g-h-t," he said just loud enough for me to hear him. Then I felt his eyes boring deep through my back and reaching to my very soul, as I walked away. For the first time in a very long time, I felt myself blush. I even started feeling a little flushed, and warm, so after I gave

135

Janisse instructions to wait on the table, I went to the restroom to cool off a bit.

Dimitri began to frequent the restaurant more and more. And even though I knew he was interested in me, he wasn't obvious with it. He was a lot more subtle than most of the men I had met, and that intrigued me. I was the fly and he was the spider who was slowly reeling me in to the sweet fragrance of his web. I had associated with and dated men who were much handsomer, and much more alluring than Dimitri, but it was his quiet confidence and refined demeanor that set him apart from other men I had known. He didn't flash his wealth or his assets. He didn't have to. But if you observed the deference and respect people paid to him whenever they saw him, it was easy to see that this was a man with power who knew how to use it with artfulness, sophistication and poise. I observed him often when he was conducting business over lunch or dinner with many of the most influential businessmen and politicians in the area, and he would listen to what the other person was saying, giving each person his undivided attention. Then, without fail, all eyes at the table would be on *him,* and all ears would be straining to hear his decisions, his counsel, his recommendations, and his pronouncements, because he never raised his voice above a certain decibel. His was a quiet, but extremely effective and powerful, diplomacy that was mesmerizing.

Then, out of the blue, one day, while I was working at the restaurant, I received a box that contained a huge, white, and wonderfully fragrant gardenia. The card read, "Wherever you are, the air around you is filled with the lasting fragrance of your inner beauty, like the matchless fragrance of this gardenia. I do hope you like it, because this exceptional, exotic flower reminds me of you." And he simply signed it "Dimitri". I couldn't stop smiling all day, and Ms. Johnston kept saying, in that part French, part American, part African, Creole language of her heritage, "Ah, Cher. Monsieur Toliver is, indeed, a most interesting man. But take your time before accepting a dance with him. He is a very powerful man, so make sure it is *you* who has the power and the control, Cher, before you begin the dance." And even though she had said it differently, it sounded like the same advice Jackie, and to some extent, Michelle, had given me in the past. So I decided to play my cards close to the hip until I really knew his intentions.

Two weeks had passed, since I'd received the gardenia, before I even saw Dimitri again. The gardenia had long since dried out, but I pressed it in a book at home, because I wanted to keep it. I didn't even see him come in the restaurant because I was back in the kitchen, helping Ms. Johnston go over some things with the chef when he arrived. "Shelley! Shelley! Are you back here?" Janisse shouted above the clanging pots in the kitchen. "I'm over here, Janisse. What's up?" I asked. "Mr. Toliver asked to speak with you," she said with a smile on her face. "Mr. Toliver? Is he here?" "Yes, he's seated at one of the private tables in the back." "How big is his party?" I asked. "He's by himself and he said he'd be dining alone," Janisse informed me. "Really? Now that's unusual. Well, go tell him I'm in a meeting and will be there just as soon as I can. In the meantime, take his order, Janisse, and make sure he's comfortable." "But, Shelley, that's just it. He said he won't order anything until he's talked with *you*." "What? Well, I wonder what *that's* about?" "Now, c'mon, Shelley. You know that man is more than interested in *you*. It doesn't take an Einstein to know *that*. And I know and you know that you're somewhat smitten by *him*, too." "Smitten? Janisse, I don't even *know* the man." "You know enough to want to know *more*, so don't even try it, Shelley. Now get on out there and find out what our customer wants, other than *you*. Isn't it *you* that's always reminding us that the customer comes first? "OK. OK. You got me, Janisse. I'm going," I said as we both laughed.

As I approached Dimitri's table, I began to get butterflies, again, in my stomach. Ol' confident Shelley Mac-

137

Donald was even a little nervous. "Ah. Here you are, at last, Shelley," he said, as if he had been waiting for me a very long time. "Well, I didn't know you had come in until just a few minutes ago, Mr. Toliver. How may I help you?" I said, professionally and formally, because it was the only way I could keep myself from saying to him, "I've missed you so much. Please don't stay away that long again." "Oh. So it's back to Mr. Toliver again? Why so formal, Shelley? I thought we were long past the Mr. Toliver stage. It's Dimitri. Remember? Dimitri. I've only been gone for two weeks and you've forgotten me that quickly?" he said, seeming to be genuinely disturbed by my detached reception. "Dimitri, of course I haven't forgotten you. I'm sorry. What can I do to make it up to you?" I said, warmly. "Whew! Now that's more like it. I thought, for a minute there that maybe the lovely, enchanting Shelley that I've grown to love had been replaced by some strange, robotic clone," he said appearing to be sincerely relieved. We both laughed for a moment. Then I said, "By the way. Thank you for that beautiful gardenia. It was exquisite. How did you know that's my favorite flower? I've never really told anyone that, nor have I been asked, come to think of it." "Somehow, I just knew, Shelley. And there's so much more that I'd like to know about you. Would you give me the honor of taking you out to dinner and, perhaps a play, or to hear some live jazz one evening? I don't think I'll have to do as much business travel as I have these past few weeks, so please just name the day and I'll make sure to clear my calendar. What do you say, Shelley?" "Dimitri. I'm more than flattered by your invitation, but I've always made it a policy not to date our customers. It just doesn't make for good business, and can cause so many unnecessary conflicts. Do you understand?" I heard myself say. "Of course. I understand, Shelley, because I operate under those same principles. So, as much as I would hate it, what if I stopped patronizing this restaurant? Would you go out with me, then?" Touché! The fragrance on the spider's web gets

138

sweeter and sweeter! "Now, Dimitri. Let's not go to extremes. You know Ms. Johnston would have my head if we lost you as a customer. I'll tell you what. Give me some time to give it some thought. Will you? In the meantime, please let me have our special for this evening brought to you. I promise you, you won't regret it." "Alright, Shelley, as long as you promise me you'll have an answer for me by, say, tomorrow, no later." "Tomorrow? Why tomorrow, Dimitri?" "Because we've waited long enough to dance. Don't you agree?" he said, staring deeply into my eyes and caressing my hand. And before I even knew what I was saying, I said, "Yes, I do."

Then he kissed my hand as if he were the Prince kissing the hand of his long, lost Cinderella. "Until tomorrow, then. Now, please may I have some food? Suddenly I feel famished!" "Oh, yes. Right away, Dimitri. I'll get your order in right away." I said, scurrying away to get his order placed. The rest of that evening, I was floating on Cloud Nine. I knew that there would be no turning back once we got together, and I no longer wanted to resist it. In fact, I was eager and somewhat curious about this graceful man who wielded such quiet power. Who was he *really*, and why did I feel so undaunted about how he would treat me? We were supposed to be together. It was as simple as that. And of that, I had no doubt.

That next evening, Dimitri and I began our dance. It was a courtship straight out of the romance novels, because he wined and dined me, of course, but he also introduced me to great jazz, the opera, the ballet, fine art, and other cultural awakenings I would never have experienced without him. But he still always kept a part of his life to himself. For instance, while he told me he was a commodities broker, and he lived the good life afforded by this profession, I was never clear about what commodity he brokered. And I didn't push the issue, because I didn't want him to think I needed to get into his personal business, as if I didn't trust him. Combine that with the fact that I didn't want this dream I was living with Dimitri to be shattered, and you'll understand why I chose to just enjoy the moment, and relish the luxury of being Dimitri's Lady. I savored the heady experience of receiving first-class treatment wherever I went because I was Dimitri's Lady. I also loved the way he interacted with Brandon, and how he comfortably took on the role of surrogate father to him. That, alone, outweighed all the accoutrements he bought me, or broadening experiences he gave me, in terms of raising my respect for and desire of him. I wanted to be with him forever, though I still had the presence of mind to keep some independence of my own, when I refused his invitation to put me and Brandon up in a condo. And even though I accepted his gifts of new furniture, etc., I still wanted to keep *my* place and *my* job, as he kept *his*.

One night, after Dimitri and I had returned to his place after dinner, he said to me, quite unexpectedly, "You know you're my lady and I wouldn't do anything to hurt you. Right?" "Yes," I said, wondering what was coming next "Well, now, I want to share something with you that I haven't shared before, because I want us to become even closer." Then he proceeded to put a mirror on the coffee table, and to pour some lines of white powder on the mirror. Then he said, "I want you to watch me carefully, Shelley, so you'll learn how to do this properly. A lot of people become sick or strung out because they don't do this right," he said as he snorted a line of cocaine up his nose. "Now I want you to look at me. Would you ever have suspected that I do this every day?" he questioned. "No. I wouldn't have, because you always seem in control and composed, unlike the crack cocaine addicts I used to see," I said, still wondering where this was leading. "Well, that's just it, Shelley. I don't use crack cocaine. This is the highest quality pure cocaine, and it makes all the difference in the world. I have never used crack cocaine, and never will. And I bet you would be shocked at the number of people who use cocaine daily, but operate and function at some of the highest levels of business, government, athletics, and the arts. If this was so harmful for you, do you think all those people would use it? No. And now, Shelley, I want you to experience and share with me this life enhancer that will have you thinking at levels and producing at levels that you'd never have believed you could. Here, watch me again before you do it, Baby." And, just as he instructed me, I watched him, carefully. Then I snorted a line of cocaine up my nose. At first, it felt foreign in my nose, and I, instinctively, wanted to blow it out. But, shortly afterward, I began to feel a high so totally superior to the highs from marijuana that I had smoked that I wondered why I had never tried it before. So that night, Dimitri initiated me into his world of cocaine, and I was an avid student. He supplied my daily bag, and I consumed it in the morning, at noon and at night, every day. In fact, we were partners who shared the pleasures of getting high together, which, we thought, elevated our intimacy to a new level.

Knock! Knock! Knock! Someone was banging on my door. "Just a moment, please. Who is it?" I asked, not expecting anyone in particular. "It's Gladys, yo' momma," the voice answered. "Momma?" I asked, thinking I had misunderstood. "Yeah, let me in Shelley, please," she said with a weak voice, almost slurring. I quickly swung the door open, and there standing before me was a woman who said she was my momma, but who really looked like an emaciated, ashy white, skeletal replica of my momma. This person really looked like *death*! "Momma? Come on in," I said, not knowing what else to say. "Sit down, Momma. Can I get you anything?" "I'd like a cold glass of water, Shelley. Can I have a cold glass of water?" "Of course, Momma. Just a minute." I got the glass of water and brought it back to her, and just stared at her as she gulped it down. "Shelley, could I take a bath or a shower here? I need to get cleaned up, but I don't have nowhere else to go." "Yes, Momma. Of course you can take a shower or bath, whichever you want, but more than that, Momma, do you want to stay here with me and let me take care of you?" I offered with no hesitation. "Can I, Shelley? Can yo' momma stay here with you? I need you now, Shelley, 'cause I don't have nowhere else to go." Then I went over and grabbed Momma and just held her tight. It was awkward, because she didn't hug me back, even though we hadn't seen each other in a long while. Then I walked her down the hall and showed her the room she could claim as her own, and started her shower water for her. While she was taking her shower, I was thinking, *Isn't it ironic that in spite of the fact that Momma turned me away when I came to her, after returning from Detroit, now she has to turn to me, because I'm now in a position to house her and help her, and that I'm doing it willingly?* So Momma came to live with Brandon and me. And, even though I knew she was still struggling with crack cocaine addiction, I welcomed her into my home. It wasn't easy, however, because I had to work, and Brandon would be with Ms. Winston all day. So that left Momma to be on her own the whole day, and I was never sure what she might be doing.

Getting ready for work one morning, I heard a car horn beeping loudly. I looked out of the window to see who was making such a racket, and there was an old, burgundy Chevrolet in front of my house. Though a car like this was very familiar to me, I didn't, in my wildest dreams, believe it belonged to the person I knew that owned a car just like that. However, the driver of the car would not stop blowing his horn. Finally, I opened my front door, and the person on the passenger side rolled his car window down and said, "There's my little girl. How ya' been doin'?" I just stood there in utter shock! I could not believe who was sitting there in the car looking at me and talking to me. All I could focus on were his yellow eyes. It was that devil, Phil! As he spoke, I watched him grimace in pain due to the loss of his skin's pigmentation. This was caused by his excessive drinking of alcohol. Next, I heard him say, "Baby Girl, c'mere!" I felt light-headed and dizzy, as if I were about to pass out. Yes, the face staring at me was the face of my so-called stepfather, and all the horrible memories of my life with him came flooding back in my mind. I hadn't seen or thought about him for years. Yet, here he was again, sitting in a car in front of my home. In a stern voice, he ordered, "Come over here and take a ride with me."

At that very moment, I lost all the strength I thought I had. I asked my neighbor to watch my son until I returned, got in the car, and sat in the back seat. He started making small talk, saying it had been a long time since we had seen each other. In a timid, soft voice I responded, "Yes, it has been." Completely out of the blue, tears began to well up in my eyes, and I dropped my head down. I felt so low, both spiritually and physically, just being in his presence. He said, "I'm lookin' for yo' momma." I lied and told him I had no idea where she was. He probed further, saying, "Are ya' sure?" I told him, "Yes, I'm sure." while thinking all along, that *I would never tell him where my mother was. Was he serious?* As we continued to drive off, I felt myself becoming enraged, to the point where a soft voice whispered to me, *If I had a gun, I'd blow his head off, right here and now!* (Thank God, I did not have a gun on me at that time, because I truly think I would have killed that man, gone to prison, and never been able to experience the joys that life might hold for me in the future.)

Shortly, thereafter, he dropped me off at home. I didn't see him after that, but I heard that he became paralyzed. I'm not sure how. "Shelley, remember I used to tell you all the time that you reap what you sow? You remember that? Well, that's what happened here to Phil. He's no longer able to move his body because he desecrated and damaged so many other people's bodies and souls. Now, I don't mean that you should wish anything *bad* on anyone, 'cause that makes *you* just as bad as *they* are. But just know that we all eventually get back what we put out. And speakin' of that, what is it that you're puttin' out now, Shelley? What is your life reflectin'? Think about that, Suga'. But I didn't come here to preach to ya', just to share some of my life's learnin's, like I always do. I just want you to find yourself, Baby, before it's too late. You're still so very young, but older than some folks twice your age. I'm just waitin' for the wisdom to kick in to match your livin' age. I love you, Shelley." And Jackie was gone, again, though her words lingered with me, especially, "I just want you to find yourself before it's too late". And, "I'm just waitin for the wisdom to kick in to match your livin' age." I couldn't get her words out of my mind, though I didn't call her back, right then, since I knew I wasn't ready to face the truth of the meaning of those words.

Momma continued to live with me, but it wasn't very long before the curtain came down on this scene in the drama of our mother/daughter lives together. A few weeks had passed, and I came home from work one evening greeted by a great deal of commotion. As I opened the door to the back room, I saw my mother with several men and women. They were all on their knees, and I saw my mother with a round, glass object in her mouth, smoking crack co-caine. I could not believe my eyes. I was speechless. My mother said, "Shelley, come down here." So, obeying my mother, I got down on my knees beside her. Then she said, "Come on. Try this." And that's exactly what I did. I felt like a little girl, again, which I really was, though I was try-ing to live a woman's life. Even though that was my first and last time smoking crack cocaine, isn't it sad that I still wanted to please my mother so much that I did exactly what she told me to do, because I was still seeking her love and acceptance? That incident made me realize that my mother's addiction was too deep to have her continue to live with me, so I asked her to leave, and she did.

At that time, Dimitri and I had also escalated our daily use of cocaine, though I never looked at myself as an addict the way I saw my mother. Of course, that's not unusual when you want to continue doing what you're doing. I was snorting so heavy that when I wasn't snorting, because I had to work, I was thinking about how good that coke felt when it reached the back of my throat. The high would numb every part of my body, so no pain could seep in. Both of us were snorting so much that we were becoming immune to the cocaine all by itself. So in order to get the high we wanted, we had to lace the cocaine with weed. Soon, Dimitri convinced me to live with him, and we got a lovely place, which we furnished with the best in designer, contemporary furniture. Eventually, when Dimitri was really high one night, while we were getting high together, he told me what commodity he brokered. Cocaine and marijuana! This refined, quietly powerful man turned out to be the top drug dealer in our area! That's what he also did in Chicago, but he had to leave there due to some business rivalries. So all the businessmen, politicians, athletes and the like that I saw him meeting were, actually, making deals to get their stuff. For some reason, I burst out laughing when he told me that, because I thought what a magnificent character actor he was, portraying refinement and culture, and all the while selling drugs—just not out in the open on the street! But this knowledge didn't make me turn away from Dimitri, like you might think it would. After all, who was I to judge *him* when I was enjoying, both literally and financially, the fruits of his labor, as evil as it was?

Dimitri and I had been living together a little under a year, when I found out I was pregnant, and, like before, the idea of abortion never entered my mind. Dimitri didn't have any children of his own, and though he was treating Brandon as if he were his son, he was really quite happy that I was having his baby. My second baby was a beautiful daughter, whom I named Lisa. She also came here very quickly, and weighed about seven pounds. So now I had two beautiful children, a son and a daughter. I was 17 years old, at the time, though I appeared older and certainly felt older. When I became pregnant with Lisa, I no longer had the desire for drugs. It was as if some spiritually-guided, automatic maternal instinct kicked in that started making me sick to my stomach at even the thought of snorting co-caine or drinking alcohol. I do believe that some divine in-tervention gave my body a magnificent purging, because, not only did I not have the desire, but also, I never had withdrawal symptoms, even though I stopped using drugs cold turkey.

No such instinct or intervention regulated Dimitri. In fact, his habit had escalated so much that he was using more drugs than he was selling. We had begun to argue, and sometimes fight practically every day. The good life that I had coveted for such a long time, suddenly started tearing apart at the seams. The ill-gotten blood money that had provided for our material lives, had no substance to sustain our spiritual lives. Then came the proverbial straw that broke the camel's back. I had taken a day off work to take my baby, Lisa, to the doctor, because I thought she might have an ear infection. Ms. Winston had to go out of town to visit her sick sister, so I asked Dimitri to watch Brandon while I was gone. He was perfectly sober, at the time, and was always good with the kids, so I was sure Brandon would be fine. When I walked in the door, after the doctor's visit, I found Dimitri strung out with one of his friends, getting high on crack cocaine, the one drug he *swore* he'd never use! Brandon was in the kitchen, pulling things out of the pantry. The kitchen floor, as well as Bran-don, was covered with flour and sugar, and I don't know what else. I was furious! What if my baby had gotten into something that could have really hurt him? Seeing Dimitri strung out like that was such a turnoff to me that my respect and love for him plummeted that very day, and I asked him to move out, which he did. About seven or eight months went by, during which time Dimitri tried to reconcile with me, but I didn't let him back. Then I didn't see him for quite a while.

It was a Friday morning, and Ms. Winston was outside loading the kids' things in her car, since she was about to take them with her for their weekend visit. The phone rang and a voice that sounded clearer than I had heard it in some time said, "Shelley, this is Dimitri. I just got back to Randall and wanted you to be the first person I talked with."

"Dimitri? Well, where have you been? It's been quite a while since we've heard from you." "I went to get help, Shelley, but instead of me telling you over the phone, do you mind if I stop by for a minute to see you and the kids? I promise I won't overstay my welcome, but I really want to see you guys." "Alright, Dimitri. Come on by," I said, curious about what his story would be.

When I opened the door and invited Dimitri in, Brandon ran to him and jumped up in his arms. He was so happy to see the only daddy he really knew. And, it was obvious that the feeling was mutual, because Dimitri was almost in tears while he was hugging both Brandon and Lisa. "They've grown so much since I last saw them, Shelley, I almost didn't recognize them. They're both so beautiful." Then he opened a shopping bag he had brought in with him and pulled out a huge, red motorized fire truck for Brandon, and a toddler-sized piano for Lisa. I almost said, "Where's mine?" as I reminisced about happier days when he was so generous to all of us. "OK, now, let's take your toys in the playroom so Daddy and Mommy can talk for a minute."

After the kids had gone to the playroom, I said, "Well how are you? You look good, Dimitri. Where have you been? It was almost like the earth had opened and swallowed you up, because no one knew where you were. Why didn't you contact us?" Then I realized I had been hurling questions at him like a machine gun shooting off. "Dimitri, I'm sorry. Where are my manners? Is there anything I can get you?" "I'd sure love a tall glass of OJ if you have it, Shelley. Thanks. And, it's OK to ask me all those questions, because you deserve to know the answers. That's one of the main reasons why I wanted to come by here first – to tell you what's been going on with me."

Then he told me that after we separated, he sunk deeper into drug abuse—so deep that he practically lost everything. And when he had hit rock bottom, and landed in jail for taking some Twinkies from a convenience store, that's when the light turned on for him about how low he had gone. He had some friends in California that he contacted and asked them to help him find a place to go to rehab. They got him out to California, and he had been in rehab all these months. And while he'd been sober for some months, he didn't want to risk coming back to Randall, or seeing me and the kids, until he was sure he would be less likely to relapse. Next he said that a friend of his here in Randall hired him to go into Sales in his business, and he had given up drug dealing and drug use forever. "I also came to ask you to forgive me, Shelley, for all the hell I put you through. My greatest regret is that I introduced you to cocaine, and if you had not gotten off that ride, I would have been responsible, and I don't think I could continue to live knowing that. Shelley, I want to try to make it up to you and the kids, and to show you that I can, once again, be worthy of your love. Please, you don't have to agree to that right now, because I know I have a lot of proving to do, and if you never give me another chance, I'll understand, but, for right now, please don't give me an answer. Let me just hope. OK?" I just smiled at Dimitri, but made no commitment to him. I was glad to see that he was making every effort to straighten out his life, but was certainly not feeling the need to make a commitment to him that I wasn't feeling at the time.

So Dimitri began to come around often and see the kids, sometimes giving me some free time by taking them to the park or the zoo. He also began surprising me, occasionally, by cooking Sunday dinner for us, or sending a box with a gardenia in it, out of the blue. Needless to say, it didn't take long for him to work his way back into our family and into my home. We started living together again, and, before long, I was pregnant for the third time. I was, truly Fertile Myrtle! We named our new baby boy Christopher, and he was also impatient to get here, to the point where the nurse had to deliver him because we couldn't get to the operating room fast enough I was 19 years old, and I was now the mother of three children. At first, things were good between Dimitri and me, and we tried hard to make a go of our relationship. But then, the arguments started, again, and we were back to fighting all the time over the most inconsequential issues. And the more we fought, the more my sexual desire for him waned, which then caused arguments about our not having sex often enough. It was a vicious cycle, and I wanted to get off the merry-go-round.

Finally, one day, I had had enough, and I got up the nerve to tell him I no longer wanted to try to have a relationship with him. What followed was a two-day nightmare! Dimitri proceeded to grab a knife, lock all the doors and windows, and pull the telephone cords from their jacks. "You think you can just leave me anytime you feel like it, and take my kids from me whenever you get the urge, Shelley? Do you think you can just use me, and take and take and take from me, then discard me like I'm a garbage bag? Well, I'll tell you who I am, Shelley, so you'll never forget it. I'm Satan, and before I let you and my kids leave me, I'll kill you all first! Do you understand me, Shelley? Do you?" Dimitri was acting like a man who had suddenly snapped and gone completely mad. He held the knife close to my neck and asked, again, in a threatening voice, "Do you understand me, Shelley?" "Yes, Dimitri, I understand you," I answered calmly. My babies were so scared, and, one by one, they began to cry. I pulled them to me and tried to quiet them down, assuring them that Daddy wouldn't hurt them. And strangely enough, I felt very calm. Maybe it was because I needed to be strong for my children. I don't really know why I stayed so unflustered, but I knew I needed to stay alert and watchful to see if I would have any opportunity to get us out of there.

The kids crying caused Dimitri to stop his haranguing long enough for me to settle them down and get them to bed. While I was doing that, at first, he was standing at the doorway of their bedrooms, watching me, still holding the knife, as if to say to me, "You'd better not try anything, either." Then he went to each of our kids' beds, and gave each of them a good-night kiss, telling them that he loved them. Finally, he followed me back into the living room, where I sat down and turned on the TV. Neither of us said a word, and the silence was deafening. Still holding the knife, he sat in a chair, adjacent to the sofa where I was sitting, and started looking at TV. Shortly thereafter, mercifully, he dozed off to sleep, still holding that knife in his hand.

This was the first night of the nightmare, and I saw his dozing off as my first opportunity to try to get us out of there. Like a lioness stalking her prey, quietly, I got up, slowly tiptoed down the stairs, opened the door, and ran to my neighbor's house, next door. My heart was beating so fast! Her front door was open, but her screen door was locked. I reached for the doorknob on her screen door, when I was suddenly yanked and dragged back to my house. It was Dimitri, and he was furious! His hand was over my mouth, so I couldn't cry out for help. He dragged me back in the house and did something he had never done to me before. He started punching me in my face. My oldest son, who had gotten out of bed, cried out, "Daddy, stop hitting my mommy!" I was even more scared that he would start on the kids, so I said, "Just go back to bed and be quiet, Baby. Mommy's OK." After a while, the rampage stopped, and we all went to bed. My face was bruised and sore, and blood was oozing from my nose. *How in the world am I ever going to get out of this?* I asked myself. *Will I ever get out of this?* my mind kept asking, not finding any answers. I lay there wide awake, beat down, forlorn, and now, totally frightened.

"Are ya' tired enough, yet, Shelley? Or the better question is, how many more of these beat downs will it take for ya' to use the good judgment and wisdom I know ya' have in ya'? Aren't ya' tired, Baby? Well, if *you* aren't, *I* sure am," Jackie said bluntly. "Now ya' got three, beautiful children to love and raise up. Do ya' want them to be raised up seein' their momma beat up and used over and over agin' 'cause she made some bad choices? I know, deep down in my soul, how ya' love your babies, Suga', so, if ya' don't want them growin' up like *you* did, seein' your momma abused by the scum of the earth, then you'd betta' make a change, Shelley, and make it now. You betta' stay alone with yourself for awhile, and heal whatever that is that you been carryin' around in you that makes ya' vulnerable to smooth-talkin', slow-walkin' men. Take some time to find out who *you* are, Shelley. I've told ya' this *before*, and, if the truth be told, I'm beginning to get tired of bein' ignored." Jackie said firmly. "And another thing, since you been makin' such bad choices, don't ya' think it's time to turn to another source to help ya', so ya' can carry a lighter load down this life's road ya' travellin'? It's time, Shelley. It's time for ya' to ask for and seek the guidance we all need on this journey. Now move on over so I can get here in the bed beside ya' and hold ya', while I tell ya' what you need to do in the mornin'." I moved over slightly and noticed how Jackie's body seemed to never change, but, still, it seemed to adjust itself comfortably to the smallest of spaces, like next to me in bed, with the greatest of ease. I was so glad to see her, and this time, I absorbed everything she said, like a sponge.

That next morning, I did exactly what Jackie had told me to do. She gave me the following words to say to Dimitri, "You know, Babe, maybe you're right. Maybe I didn't give us enough time to work things out, so we could make it as a family. So, let me go to the grocery store and get some food, and I'll make us a good breakfast for the whole family. That will be a good, fresh start for us. What do you say?" "Take Lisa and Chris with you to the store, and leave Brandon here with me, " he said, sounding like the *sane* Dimitri I knew. So off we went to the grocery, and, just as Jackie had told me to do, I immediately went to the police. And they quickly went to my home and arrested

Dimitri. As he was being handcuffed, he stared at me with eyes that were filled with disbelief that I would send the police after him. So I guess I answered Jackie's questions. Yes, I had had *enough*! And that was the last I heard or saw of Dimitri for a time. Some years later, I heard that he had gotten married and was doing well with a new family of children, and I was happy to hear that, for his sake, because our dance should have ended long before it did. We had been dancing, all those years, on a dance floor made of clay, rather than the solid rock foundation that we really needed to have a good life together.

Chapter 11

After the ordeal with Dimitri, I was totally spent, exhausted, drained, run down, fatigued, worn out, and empty, both physically and mentally. I had nothing left in me to give to anyone, even my children. I needed to unravel the mystery of where my life was going, and how, as a nineteen year-old, single mother of three young children, I was going to be able to give them a good life. The one thing I knew was that my children would always be my priority. But I needed to sort out who I was, and why my life kept following the same, destructive patterns that ended up in hurt and pain, emotionally, physically and financially. *What's wrong with me that keeps me making the same mistakes over and over again?* I kept asking myself, perplexed by the turns my life had taken. But I was, literally, too tired to even think. I just wanted some peace. "Take some time off to rest, Cher. Use my cabin at the lake for a week and refresh and restore yourself. Take a retreat with your spirit, Ma Petite, because you have a lot of responsibility weighing on those small shoulders of yours that you must find a way to carry," Ms. Johnston counseled. So I took her up on her offer, and luckily, Mother Winston, (we had gotten so close that Ms. Winston insisted on me and the kids calling her Mother Winston, now) was more than happy to take them for a week, so I could get away.

Ms. Johnston's cabin was on a private lake, surrounded by hills lined with tall, leafy green trees of every kind. The lake was the deepest blue I had ever seen.. I had never been anyplace as quiet and tranquil as this place was. And even though Ms. Johnston had appointed this secluded cabin with modern amenities like electricity, plumbing, television and the like, it still was the ideal environment to get away, commune with nature, and be alone with oneself. The first day I got there, I slept for practically the whole day. The same was true of Day 2. All the years of turmoil and turbulence in my life had finally caught up with me and all I could do was sleep. "It's alright, Baby Girl. Just you rest, now," Jackie said softly, as she held me on her lap and rocked me in the rocking chair. "Yes, I called ya' Baby Girl, again, 'cause that's what you need ta' be, right now. Ya' need to be my Baby Girl, free from any worries, hurt, pain, disappointment or burdens, so you can get the fullness of the rest ya' need. Ya' need to clean out yo' head and yo' heart and relieve it of the burdens of yo' past. So be free as a baby, right now, Little One, and go to sleep," she said, humming that song that still sounded so familiar to me. And, at that moment, I felt like a little child being loved, embraced and comforted by her momma, drifting off to a deep and restful sleep.

I awakened the next morning hearing someone say on the television, "Follow along with me as I read what Jesus said, in Matthew, Chapter 11, verse 28: Come unto me, all ye that labor and are heavy laden, and I will give you rest." I didn't even remember turning on the television, so I wondered if Jackie had turned it on and just forgot to turn it off before she left. Thinking no more about it, I went into the bathroom, and started running water in the tub. I noticed that there were several bottles of bubble bath around the huge tub, with different fragrances. I picked one, poured some in the tub, and ran my hands through the soothing wa-

154

ter as I watched the tub fill up with beautiful bubbles. Then I saw a container of bath salts, and added some to the water, as well. Finally, I lit several of the candles that were in the room, and turned out the light. Steam was filling the room carrying with it the floral fragrance of lilacs, as I slipped down into the tub as far as I could, letting the warm water and bubbles totally envelope me. I was in absolute heaven. And I drifted off into a blissful sleep.

All week, I totally indulged myself by sleeping as much as I wanted to, eating as much as I wanted to, from the refrigerator full of food that Ms. Johnston had the caretaker fill before I arrived, taking long, causal walks in the woods and sitting for hours, looking out over the calm waters of the lake. I was completely alone for maybe the first time in my entire life, other than when Jackie came to visit me. I thoroughly enjoyed, and didn't resent Jackie being there with me, because, unlike former visits where she usually was sharing some of her "life's learnin's" with me to teach me some valuable lesson, this time she came basically just to be with me, and encourage me to rest and be still. "Ya' don't need to worry yourself, right now, about what to do next, Shelley, Baby, because those answers will come to ya' when they need to. And you'll figure out who ya' are in due time. Just let yourself go within and dwell there for a spell, while you rest," she told me in the most comforting, warm and loving voice I had heard from her in a while. "Trust me. Things will fall into place, as they should." So I did. I relaxed, I rested, and I trusted Jackie, the one constant in my life.

The week flew by quickly, and, though I could have stayed longer, I became anxious to see my kids. When I got home, I was met with a week-old pile of mail containing a mountain of bills that needed to be paid. That meant that they had to be paid by me alone, since Dimitri was no longer there to share the expenses. But, strangely enough, I didn't panic or become distressed. There was a new tranquility that dominated my attitude and outlook about life, now, so I put the bills in a stack on the counter and proceeded to call Mother Winston to let her know I was home and wanted to see my children. When Brandon and Lisa walked in the door, and Mother Winston came in carrying Chris in her arms, the sight of my children made me realize that one of my great purposes in life was to be the absolute best mother to these children I could be. "Mommy!" they all yelled jumping on me and hugging me, "I missed you!" they said, almost in unison. "Not as much as I missed you," I said, kissing all of them as we hugged. Then Mother Winston went back out to her car and brought in a platter of fried chicken, a pot of greens, a pot of mashed potatoes and gravy, and some of her good, ol' sweet cornbread. So we all had dinner together, and I was the happiest I had been in recent memory.

When I went back to work, I thanked Ms. Johnston for the use of her cabin, and she said, "Any time, Cher. We women have to play so many roles that we sometimes forget to take care of ourselves. So, from now on, you make sure you plan at least a day's retreat for yourself, once a month. And on that day, you can choose to pamper yourself for a whole day at a spa, read a good book all day, or go away to be alone to rest or meditate, whatever is your pleasure. You must clear away the cobwebs of life, every now and then, to enjoy the fruits of life. So promise me you'll do that, Shelley." "I promise, Ms. Johnston, and thanks again." So I was back at work, and life for me and my children began to settle into a routine and rhythm.

But I kept feeling that something was missing from it. And that something missing had nothing to do with a man, because I had soured on the idea of wanting to pursue a relationship with a man anytime in the foreseeable future. I was neither lonely nor hungry to have a man in my life. No, it was something else that was absent from my life, and I somehow knew I was on the brink of discovering what that was. I also knew, by some means, that once I made that discovery, I would eventually find all the answers about

156

myself and about my life that I had repeatedly been asking myself over the years. The one thing that I *had* identified and realized about myself, as I quietly walked in the woods at the cabin, or sat beside that magnificent, cerulean lake, was that there was something *different* about me—different in a *good* way, not different in the way that consumed my past. I also remembered that from the time I was nine-years old and wanted to stay in church all day, every day because of the love and spirit I experienced there, I felt, with no apparent evidence of same, that my life would matter in some way, and that there was greatness in me. Then the words of that preacher who was on TV one morning at the cabin kept filling my head, over and over again, "Come to me." "Come to me..." I couldn't get those words out of my mind.

It was the weekend, and I was scheduled to work at the restaurant from the dinner hour until 11:00 p.m. all weekend. The kids were at Mother Winston's for the weekend, as usual. It was about 4:00 a.m., and I had had a restless night, for some reason, when I was suddenly bolted out of bed by hearing someone say to me as clearly as if they were standing right beside me, "COME TO ME!" in what seemed a fairly loud voice. I quickly turned on the lamp on the night stand, and slowly got out of bed, putting on my robe. "Is someone there?" I yelled. Then, I realized that was a stupid thing to do, because I didn't know what I'd do if it was someone who had broken in, and they suddenly answered, "Yes!" But no one answered. I slowly and carefully went into the hallway and turned on the light. Then I cautiously tiptoed to every single room and turned on the lights, so it ended up with all the lights in my entire home fully lit. But there was no one there to be found. *I must have been dreaming*, I thought as I turned off all the lights, and got back in bed. After that, I dropped off into a deep and restful sleep.

The next morning, I showered, and as I was drying myself off, I heard, "I saw you walkin' around the house this morning, Baby. You were scared, weren't you?" Jackie asked. Then I proceeded to tell her what had happened, and how clear the voice that I heard sounded to me. She smiled and said, "Shelley, the words that you heard this voice say, Come to me, had you ever heard them before?" "Well, yeah. I heard a preacher read them from the Bible on television one morning at the cabin. The sound of the TV had woke me up, and that's what I heard. But I don't remember turning the TV on the night before. Did you leave it on?" "I could have," Jackie answered, with a slight smile on her face. "But you know what else is so weird about it, Jackie? Lately, those very same words, Come to me, have been going through my mind over and over again. Isn't that creepy?" "It may seem that way right now, Suga', but I do know this. The mind, where you been hearin' these words over and over, is the place where the soul dwells. And the soul is the place where your Spirit dwells. And, most important, my Sweet, the Spirit is the place where God dwells. They all work together, ya' see? So when yo' Spirit is tryin' to tell you something, it will inhabit your mind and yo' soul 'til you get it. Even if ya' put the message out of yo' mind for a time, because ya' don't wanna' hear it, it will eventually keep comin' back to ya'. Now, what you heard at 4:00 a.m. this mornin' was indeed a voice that you will come to recognize if ya' really want to. I believe it came to ya' that way because, even though your mind was being filled with the same message, you weren't gettin' it fast enough, and this is a *right now* message, Shelley Baby." "So do you mean that was God's voice I heard, Jackie? And what does He mean by, Come to me?" "Shelley, you have to find out all these things for yourself, Baby. But trust me. If you really want to find out, you'll start lookin' for the answer until you find it. Listen, cain't nobody else really find the meaning of the message that was meant for *you*, but *you*, Sweetie. Now, come on over here and give me my hug, Darlin'. I gotta' go now, but I'll see you agin' soon." After Jackie left, I kept going over what

she had told me, and even though I only half-way under-
stood everything she said, and only half-way believed that
it was God's voice that awoke me, I was still curious
enough to want to know for sure.

"Shelley, when's the last time you read the Bible, or
even went to church?" Mother Winston asked me, after I
phoned her and told her about what had happened to me.
"It's been a long time, Mother Winston," I told her. "Well,
I'm not tryin' to push ya' into somethin' ya' not ready to
do, but it seems ta' me that you might want to consider
goin' to church with me and the kids in the morning. Could
be, that might be a start to yo' findin' yo' answers. And if it
ain't, then at least you tried. Whatta' you say? At the very
least, it would be good for the children to see their momma
in church with 'em." "What time does church start, Mother
Winston?" I asked. "Well, me and the kids go to the 11:00
service. Why don't we swing by and pick you up at 10:15,
and that would give us plenty of time to get there on time."
"OK. Mother Winston. I'll be ready. Now let me talk to my
little monsters," I said laughing.

That Sunday began my journey of self-discovery about
who I am, whose I am, and why I'm here. By the time
Bishop Norton had finished her sermon, and gave the invitation to accept Jesus Christ, or to rededicate our lives to
Him, my face was drenched with tears, as if I was mourn-
ing for the lost years that had past when I had separated
myself from God. I almost *ran* up to the altar and got down
on my knees thanking God for not giving up on me, even
though I had not been seeking Him. Then I felt gentle
hands and arms helping me up, and wiping away my tears,
and it was Jackie and some of the ministers of the church.
After that, I became hungry for the Word of God, and
thirsty for what He was teaching me. I was obsessed with a
desire to have a relationship with Him. Instead of trying to
complete myself with men, I only felt complete when I was
with Him. I poured over the Bible voraciously, seeking an
understanding about my life. And I started asking questions

at Bible Study, and, eventually, became comfortable enough to ask the Bishop questions, one-on-one, trying to get clarity. Then I began to serve in the church in different capacities, eager to do whatever needed to be done. I was a baby in Christ who was on fire for the Lord.

One evening, Ms. Johnston introduced me to a new employee she had contracted for the restaurant whose name was Steve Williams. She had hired him from one of the fine dining restaurants in Baltimore, which was a competitor of ours. Always the businesswoman, Ms. Johnston wanted to expand the restaurant further on the surrounding property and needed someone to oversee that whole project, from architectural design through complete construction of the expansion. Steve was quite handsome, and he had the cutest smile. But, I was not interested one little bit in disrupting the flow of my life, at that point, by having a man intrude on it. "Shelley, you're gonna end up an old maid if you don't start getting' out and enjoyin' life. Now, that sweet hunk of mocha chocolate over there, *Steve*, he might be *the one*, Shelley. But you so uptight, you too blind to see a good thing if It was standing smack dab in front of you," Janisse said, laughing. "Girl, I don't have the time, nor the desire, to fool with no man. I've been with enough of them, with three kids to prove it, to last me a lifetime. Me and my kids are doin' just fine, thank you, and I intend for it to stay that way. Capiche?" "Tsk, Tsk, Tsk! Yeah, I capiche alright. I capiche that you been bitten so much by the *wrong* men, that you scared to even consider that there is a *right* man out there for you." "Look, Janisse. I know you and Jerry have been married for some years and have made it a good marriage, but it doesn't happen that way for everybody. OK? I'm happy for you, though, and if I had a man that loved me the way Jerry loves *you*, I'd believe it could happen to others too. I just think it wasn't in the cards for me, and I've accepted that and made a good life for me and the kids on my own." "OK, Shelley. But you know I love you, and I can't help wanting to see you find somebody that will love you and support you like you deserve." "Thanks, Girl. I love you too, and I appreciate your wanting the best for me."

"Shirley? Could you help me a minute, please? Could you help me find the old blueprints for the restaurant in Ms. Johnston's office. She told me where they were, but I still can't find them, and was unable to reach her on the phone," Steve came up to me and asked that next day. "Oh, sure. She told me where they are. Come on with me. And, by the way. The name is Shelley, not Shirley," I said. "Oh, I'm so sorry, Shelley. I'm just terrible with names. But I promise you, I won't forget it from now on," Steve said with the cutest smile. "Well, you just make sure you don't!" I said, firmly, feigning anger. At first, Steve thought I was really angry, and I almost pulled it off, but when he started to apologize so sincerely to me, again, I burst out laughing. Then he looked at me and started laughing too. "You got me that time. But I'll know better next time," he said, with the cutest smile. "We'll see," I said, suddenly realizing that I was slightly flirting with him, which came as a total sur-prise to me. Then I gave the blueprints to Steve, and went back to managing the early dinner hour.

That began a friendship with Steve that became fun for me. He had the greatest sense of humor and we were al-ways laughing about something. We even joked about some of the women who worked in both the restaurant and Ms. Johnston's office, who made it very clear that they had the hots for him. One day, Steve asked me what church I attended, because he had been visiting churches, but hadn't yet decided where he would join. I told him about my church, and invited him to meet us there that Sunday, which he did. And he continued to do so, until he joined within that same month. As it turned out, Steve was a God-fearing man, as well as, an all around great guy. I found myself looking forward to seeing him both at work and at church, because we had developed a great friendship. I had never had a male friend before, so this was a new experience for me.

"Listen. I've got some tickets to see Anita Baker in concert next week. Why don't we make a night of it and go out to dinner before the concert," Steve asked. "Are you serious? What happened to Beverly?" I asked. "Did you guys break up?" "I don't know how that rumor got started, but Beverly and I were *never* together in the *first* place. We went out for *one* dinner, *one* dinner, and now I hear we're a *couple*. Believe me that is not the case," Steve said, sounding a little irritated. "Look, Shelley. I'm asking you, because it's *you* I want to be with. And I kinda thought you were beginning to feel the same about me. Am I right?" "Yes! Uh No! Listen, Steve, we are good friends, and I don't know if I'm ready, right now, for us to be anything else. I love you as my friend, and I don't want to lose that." "But that's just it, Shelley. You've become my *best* friend, and I know, now, that I want that relationship with *whatever* woman God sends me to spend the rest of my life with. It's a great foundation for an even deeper relationship, which is, frankly, what I want to have with *you*. I'm asking you out on a *date*, Shelley MacDonald, that I pray will be the first of many dates to come, because I'm beginning to care for you even deeper than our friendship goes. Now, I know what you've been through in the past, but I'm not those men, Shelley. And you *know* I'm not. So let's take it one day at a time, and just see where this takes us. That's all I'm asking. I promise you. I won't rush you or hurt you. But I *will* be persistent, young Lady. I'm telling you that up front. So, how about it? Dinner and the concert next week. Do we have a date?" And that began a courtship that lasted for two years, following what had been two years of dating abstinence.

Steve attended church with me and the kids every Sunday and Tuesday. He also was quite the romantic, because he treated me like a queen, sending me flowers "out of the blue," giving me presents, like diamond earrings "just because," I was floating on a cloud. Finally, I had found my knight in shining armor, who also loved the Lord! When Steve asked me to marry him, I felt absolutely no hesitation in saying, "YES!" And though life presented us some bumps in the road along the way, we weathered those storms together, which brought us even closer. We both agreed that it was important for us to receive pre-marital counseling from the Bishop. So we completed our counseling sessions and then the Bishop married us.

We picked the perfect day to marry, because the sky was sunny and blue and full of puffy white cumulus clouds. I was so excited, because, for the first time in many years, my whole family would be together. My mother, Gladys, Mother Winston, Ms. Johnston and my maid of honor, who was my best friend, were in the Bridal Room helping me get dressed. Yes, my mother was finally whole again, and was clucking around me like a mother hen, and I was loving every minute of it. My dad had also flown in from Detroit to walk me down the aisle. And my brothers Greg and Derrick, and my sister, Dorothy were also in the wedding. My beautiful children would be taking part too. Then, the ceremony was about to begin, so everyone left the room to take their places. I was in the room all by myself, and as I was examining myself in the mirror, I began to see myself in all the stages of my life, from the terrified and abused little three-year-old, to the raped seven-year old, to the abandoned 13-year old, to the abused 15-year-old young mother, and on and on. Tears started streaming down my face as I reflected on how God had brought me through all of that pain to this place of sacred love that I was beginning today. The tears were for the hurt and pain and fear that I had to go through, but they were also tears of absolute and total joy that God had loved me enough to bring me to this point.

"Shelley, Baby. I know why ya' cryin' 'cause I've already used up one box of tissues myself just standin' here lookin' at my beautiful Baby Girl becomin' a righteous woman of God through the sanctity of this marriage, and through your relationship with Him. I been cryin' 'cause I'm so very happy for you, Baby, but not only because of what's happenin' here today. Ya' see, very soon, all the questions that you've had about why you went through so many struggles and hardships in your life will be answered, 'cause God's gonna reveal to you what His purpose is for the rest of your life. You'll see. Mark my words." Jackie said. "Ah, you look absolutely beautiful, my Sweet, but let's dry those tears and freshen up this makeup before we get out there," Jackie said, while applying blush to my cheeks with a makeup brush. "Jackie, will you walk down the aisle with me too? I want you to walk me down the aisle, opposite my dad, 'cause you've been everything to me all my life." "Oh, Baby, I thought you'd never ask. You know I will 'cause I'll always be with ya'. Now, let's go. They're playin' the Wedding March just for you."

As we entered the sanctuary, my heart began to burst with gratitude and rejoicing that the Lord had brought me to this special place. I looked over at Jackie, and she flashed me that brilliant smile that accentuated her perfect cheek bones. She was absolutely beautiful, and she hadn't aged a bit in all these years. I made a mental note, walking down that aisle, to ask Jackie what was her secret to the fountain of youth,' cause I might need it one day. (Now isn't that just like a woman to be thinking of how to pre-serve her youth while she's walking down the aisle to be joined to her future husband? We women are interesting creatures, and it sure is a blessing to have God love us, anyhow!)

We exchanged our vows, and before Bishop said, "You may now kiss your bride," she said, "Brandon, Lisa and Christopher, please come and stand in front of your mother and father." When the children came forward, to my com-plete surprise, Steve knelt down in front of them, and Bishop consecrated him as their *spiritual* father, because he wanted to adopt them as such. And then he put his arms around all three of my children, now *our* children, and hugged them close. I was so overcome with joy that I could barely contain myself, and when Bishop said, "You may now kiss your bride," I kissed that man so hard and so deep and so long that after clapping, everyone began laughing, including Steve and me. Someone even yelled, "Shelley, let the man up for air!" It was the most beautiful experience I've ever had, and I thanked God for sending me this wonderful man.

Ms. Johnston insisted on giving us the wedding reception free at Antoinette's. It was truly grand. She had decorated the restaurant all in white, silver and lilac, and had tons of flowers as far as the eye could see. The table centerpieces were gorgeous and among other beautiful flowers, she included my favorites, gardenias and lilacs. The air was filled with their fragrance. Ms. Johnston even had contracted a live band. And, of course, the food was beyond delicious. As I was walking from table to table, talking with all the guests, I walked over to Momma, who was holding my brother Greg's new baby boy. As I drew closer, I could hear Momma humming and singing to the baby, as she rocked him. As I listened, I recognized that it was the same lullaby Jackie hummed to me over the years. "Momma," I said, in a low voice, so I wouldn't wake the baby, "what's that song you're singing?" "Shelley, it's "Blessed Child – God's Own Treasure." Don't you remember? I used to sing it to you all the time when you were a baby, and you wouldn't go to sleep until I did. Don't you remember?" And suddenly, I did. I remembered Momma holding me in her arms, rocking me, as she sang that lullaby to me. That's why it had sounded familiar to me, all along. "Yeah, Momma. I remember now. I love you." "I love you too, Shelley," Momma said. And as I hugged her, I knew that she did.

After I had been under Bishop's teaching at the church for about two years, I started feeling a tugging and stirring in my spirit. I knew it was God compelling me to do something, but I just couldn't identify what the something was. Then, early one morning, at about 3:00 a.m. I heard the Lord say to me, "FEED MY SHEEP." I was so scared. I said, "God, please, I beg you. Choose someone else. I don't have the education." And I proceeded to point out to God all the other reasons why I wouldn't qualify for such an awesome task, as if He didn't already know everything about me, better than I knew myself. I didn't get a response from God after my pleas. So I sat down, not knowing what to do. I thought to myself, *I barely know anything about the Bible, because it's still so new_to me. I'm not a Bible scholar, by a long shot.* Then I went back to my room and opened up the Bible. I didn't know what to look for. I was so confused. So, I asked the Lord, "Who's going to believe this, and what am I supposed to do now?" As clear as day, I heard the Lord say to me, "SIT DOWN AND BE TAUGHT!" I had learned to keep a journal, and I wrote down everything the Lord had said to me in that journal. Unlike the very first time I heard God's voice telling me "COME TO ME," because I had given over my life to Him, and was building a personal relationship with Him, I now recognized his voice, just as Jackie had told me I would a few years ago. The next day, when I went to work, I took a small, blue Gideon's Bible to work with me. This was a Bible that I had taken from a hotel room years ago, and I still have that same Bible today. (The Lord works in mysterious ways.) While I was on my breaks and at lunchtime, I began reading the Bible. I turned to the Gospel of Matthew, the 21st Chapter, and read the whole chapter that day. I also began reading the Gospel of John. I was reading in the 21st Chapter of John, at the 17th verse, when I read where Jesus told Peter, "FEED MY SHEEP." I read that same verse over and over, because I couldn't believe, at first, what I was reading. *This can't be what I heard the Lord say to me, can it?* I asked myself. You see, I had never seen nor read nor heard this passage before in the Bible, until then. That's how much I was still such a baby in Christ. I kept this whole encounter with God quiet in my spirit, because I didn't think anyone would believe me. The only person I told about it was Jackie. "Jackie, I know I heard God say this to me, but I don't understand why." I said, searching for answers. "Don't fret, Suga'. You'll know when you know. And it will be at the right time. Trust me." And I did.

For two years, I kept my month shut until the Lord pressed down on my spirit for me to tell the Bishop about what He had told me to do. . Being obedient, one day I went to the Bishop and I said "Bishop I know this is going to sound strange, and, at the same time, a bit crazy. I don't even understand it myself, but the Lord told me to "FEED HIS SHEEP." She just looked at me and said, "Go back and pray about it," and that's what I did. I waited another six months, until I couldn't take it any longer. I felt like I was burning inside with such a compulsion to preach God's Word that I asked God, "What else should I do'?" So the Lord answered me. Shortly thereafter, I said to the Bishop, in a soft, respectful voice, "Bishop, the Lord has called me to FEED HIS SHEEP." She just looked at me and smiled, but as I started to walk out of the sanctuary, she touched my shoulder, and then she confirmed my calling. "I've been praying about you and observing you for some time, Shelley. That's why I have been teaching you and showing you many more things than I usually do, preparing you for this day. Yes, the Lord has called you to preach, and you must obey Him," Bishop said. I was excited, nervous and shocked, all at the same time. Bishop took me under her wing, after that, and began teaching me what I needed to know. She licensed me as a minister in 2002.

Bishop walked up to me one day and said, "Shelley, you need to go to Seminary and study to prepare yourself further for the ministry. I've already told the Seminary that I'm sponsoring you, but you need to schedule an appointment with them for an interview and get registered to begin your studies." I began to panic. Studying at Seminary meant I would be doing college level work. When I got in my car, I cried out, "Lord, how am I going to go to Seminary when I don't even have my GED?" But He didn't answer me.

I scheduled my first interview and was then called back for several more interviews. The Bishop had written a great recommendation for me, but I thought, *God, it will truly take one of your divine miracles to get me accepted in this Seminary, and continued miracles for me to successfully complete the course of study. But I know that you called me, and I trust you.*

My final interview was with a lady in Admissions, who would give the final approval for me to be accepted as a student. I remember her to this day. After our interview, she said to me, "I normally would not do this, because you don't have a high school education, let alone any college experience, but, there is *something* about you that makes me know you'll do fine here." Well, even though I hadn't been nervous about this in the spirit, I still almost passed out with disbelief in the flesh. God did indeed answer me, big time! He took Shelley Williams (my married name), with only a 6th grade formal education, and placed her in a college level seminary so He could give her further preparation for what He had called her to do. So, I matriculated for three years and graduated from the Seminary with a degree in Pastoral Studies. And because God had seen to it that I received my degree from Seminary, He also saw to it that I received my GED, as well, for which I did not have to take courses, since I had already completed college level work. From that point on, I have *never*, to this day, doubted that anything can happen if the Lord wills it so.

"God is able. He *is* all things. He *knows* all things. He can *do* all things. And yet, as holy and omnipotent as He is, His heart melts with love for each and every one of us, His children. He's faithful in His love for us, and as BIG as God is, He *still* wants an intimate and personal relationship with *each* of us. His plan for our lives is filled with love, peace, prosperity and all that is good and righteous. And He *never* gives up on us, even though we sometimes turn our backs on *Him*. I've told you all about my life. I am one of God's *miracles*! I am alive today because He *saved* me. I would be nothing today without God. He loved me so much that He brought me through sexual abuse, poverty, abandonment, drug abuse, teenage pregnancy, and domestic abuse, and more than one near-death experience, so that I could be a witness to His power, mercy and grace. But, that gift is not uniquely given to *me*, Shelley Williams. It is there for *all* of us. And He makes it so *simple*. It is a choice that we make to accept Jesus Christ as our Lord and Savior, and the doors of salvation are open to *all* of us. So now I extend that invitation to *you*. If *you* are seeking peace beyond understanding, immeasurable and unconditional love, rest from your burdens and struggles, come to this altar right now and accept Jesus," I said, as I was ending my sermon.

Suddenly, I saw a little girl stand up in the back of the church. She was crying, and she started walking up the aisle, tentatively. Her father reached out for her and said, "Come back here!" "Do not stop this child. Let her come!" I commanded. I came down from the pulpit, and started walking toward her, and as I did, this little girl started to look like *me*, on the day I walked down the aisle and accepted Jesus in my life when I was nine years old. For a brief moment I closed my eyes, and when I opened them, it was the little girl again, not me, but I discerned in my spirit that she was being abused in her home the same way that *I* had been, at her age. Then I saw Jackie, who had taken the little girl's hand and was walking with her towards me, nodding her head, as she looked at me, acknowledging that my discernment about this little girl's suffering was correct. Jackie was dressed all in luminous white, the same way she looked on the day that *I* accepted Jesus Christ. And there seemed to be rays of light radiating all around her, exactly like they did on that special day for *me*, so many years ago.

They had almost reached me, when I saw the little girl look up and smile at Jackie. I felt a tear trickle down one side of my face, because I was overjoyed that this precious little girl would have Jackie with *her*, as she had been with me, to carry her through. Jackie looked down at the little girl with a smile and winked her eye, as they continued to walk towards me. When they reached me, I knelt down in front of the little girl and embraced her, as I welcomed her into the fullness of the love of God, while Jackie embraced us both.

CPSIA information can be obtained
at www.ICGtesting.com
Printed in the USA
BVHW080451080319
542139BV00001B/60/P